D1377117

Praise for TRUST IN THE LORD: REFLECTIONS OF JESUS CHRIST

The book is gripping. I turned to it early one Sunday morning and did not stop until I finished the last page. It is so personal, so heartfelt, so insightful, and so beautifully written.   —Richard L. Bushman,
author and professor of history, Columbia University

The book is absolutely wonderful! Each page is insightful and inspiring and will undoubtedly strengthen and encourage those who read the book. I believe it will make a real difference in the lives of many.   —Gary L. Crittenden, *Chief Financial Officer of CitiGroup*

Deen Kemsley has written an inspiring study of how Christ works in people's lives to bring them to Himself, and to guide them throughout their lives, which is based almost entirely on central principles shared with all major branches of Christianity. With riveting personal illustrations punctuating the volume, the book should benefit readers from many different backgrounds, even as they might take issue with a handful of points here or there. I found the work personally uplifting and encouraging!   —Craig Blomberg, *distinguished professor of New Testament, Denver Seminary*

This is an inspiring, uplifting book. I enjoyed it immensely. It is written in an ecumenical manner which I believe will appeal to a broad audience, drawing readers closer to God. I could feel the Spirit of the Lord as I read it, and I felt closer to Him. The world needs this book!
—David Neeleman, *founder of Jet Blue Airways*

I thoroughly enjoyed this book. It contains many lessons and insights that I found edifying, thought-provoking, and inspirational. I look forward to sharing this book with my family and friends.
—Rick Chamiec-Case, *faculty, Calvin Christian College*

I love the book! In fact, some of the most stirring, touching words I have ever read are in this book. I truly believe the world needs this book. —Richard Rust, *author and professor of English, University of North Carolina at Chapel Hill*

Deen Kemsley is an even better man than author. Yet that fact is exactly what qualifies him to write this simple yet beautiful work. I recommend it to all! —David W. Checketts, *former CEO of Madison Square Garden, and president of the New York Knicks*

The concepts in this book are fresh and rich, beautifully illustrated with personal stories and well-executed summaries of Christ's life. It has a calming effect that will bring tranquility and living water to the parched among us in these turbulent times. I loved the author's stories, and I loved the flow. This is a very important book! —Rodney Jay Vessels, *author*

Honest, passionate, and enlightening . . . Kemsley's *Trust in the Lord* is a timely collection of insights that uplift and reassure those seeking to understand life's trials. —Jeff Benedict, *author*

This book is a must-read for all who may be having trouble keeping their earthly priorities straight. I can't think of anyone who wouldn't benefit from reading Deen Kemsley's words, stories, and reflections on what it means to truly follow the Savior, even Jesus Christ.
—Rodney A. Hawes Jr., *philanthropist and donor for Hawes Hall at Harvard Business School*

Using beautiful language, Deen testifies of the strength Christ can provide to us through life's ups and downs. The book will surely inspire every reader.
—James H. Quigley, *global CEO of Deloitte Touche Tohmatsu*

Trust in the *Lord*

Reflections of Jesus Christ

By Deen Kemsley

Sweetwater Books
Springville, Utah

ISBN 13: 978-1-59955-114-2

Published by Sweetwater Books, an imprint of Cedar Fort, Inc., 2373 W. 700 S., Springville, UT, 84663
Distributed by Cedar Fort, Inc., www.cedarfort.com

LIBRARY OF CONGRESS CATALOGING-IN-PUBLICATION DATA

Kemsley, Deen, 1957–
  Trust in the Lord : reflections of Jesus Christ / Deen Kemsley.
    p. cm.
  ISBN 978-1-59955-114-2 (alk. paper)
  1. Jesus Christ—Mormon interpretations. 2. Trust in God—Christianity. I. Title.

BX8643.J4K46 2007
232—dc22
                              2007040610

Cover design by Nicole Williams
Cover design © 2008 by Lyle Mortimer
Edited and typeset by Lyndsee Simpson Cordes

Printed in the United States of America

10 9 8 7 6 5 4 3 2 1

Printed on acid-free paper

I dedicate this book to the common bond of Christ that unites us together in the comfort and peace of his redeeming grace.

Table of Contents

Acknowledgments

As I wrote, I often found myself reflecting on the words of C. S. Lewis, whom I acknowledge. His conversion to Christ resonates with me, as does his emphasis on the common voice we all hear whenever Christ speaks to our hearts, regardless of religious sect or denomination. In addition, I acknowledge the impact of the Reverend Marion Law, rector of St. Paul's Church in Pawtucket, Rhode Island, from 1896 to 1917. Although his books are out of print and long forgotten by most, they are deeply meaningful to me, for they are filled with love for Christ. Finally, I recognize the influence of Ralph Waldo Emerson, whose essays captivated me when I was young and still strengthen me today.

More directly, I rely heavily upon the words of Christ himself, as recorded in the Holy Bible. Each chapter draws upon this sacred volume. Whenever I allude to specific words of the Savior, I use the King James Version of the text.

I also acknowledge the encouragement and advice I received from Richard Rust; Jeff Benedict; Craig Bloomberg; Richard Mouw; Gerald McDermott; Rod Vessels; Rick Chamiec-Case; Norene Killpack; my parents, Bill and Jackie Kemsley; my brothers, Mark and Keith; and my sisters, Vicki and Cathi. Most of all, I express gratitude to my wife, Kristin, and to the many friends and family members in whom I have seen Christ reflected many times over the years. In this book, I share a few of these reflections of Christ.

Author's Note

Just north of Tulane University is a three-story apartment building on Fontainebleau Drive. Like many homes in New Orleans, the building looks charming from the outside. Inside it just looks old. The hall lights seldom work, doors are hard to open, and nameless creatures scurry through the walls. When I teach at Tulane University, I stay in a second-floor apartment in this building. Although the place isn't much, I love it deeply because it's the spot I began writing this book. After years of writing academic research papers, I set my evenings in New Orleans aside for this new endeavor, an endeavor that allowed me to reflect on the great sacrifice Jesus Christ made for us.

When Hurricane Katrina slammed into New Orleans in August of 2005, I had not yet finished the book. The storm flooded the apartment building. Mold spread throughout, and contractors had to strip the entire first floor of the building to its studs. Therefore, I had to finish the book in retreat back home in Connecticut.

The theme of the book is the journey to know Christ is the journey to know the deepest, best element of ourselves. If we embrace this divine element within us by genuinely believing in Christ, we experience the wonder of being born of God, and we discover that Christ's power to heal is deeper than our deepest pain.

My sole intent is to prompt readers to look within themselves to find the light and peace of Jesus Christ, the only name under heaven through which we can be saved. To do so, I share personal anecdotes, observations, and reflections that reveal momentary glimpses into the power of Christ's redeeming grace—the foundation for all our joy. My memory isn't what it used to be, so I'm not sure all of these experiences occurred exactly as I've described them. However, I've described them as accurately as I could. There is no error in the central message I convey, which is that God is there, he hears our prayers, and he loves us.

one

EVIDENCE OF CHRIST

God is there, he hears our prayers, and he loves us.

$\mathcal{A}$ small pond sits at the bottom of the hill behind my home. One cold December night, I walked down to the pond alone. At the time, I faced a crisis in my career. After several years of intense struggle and effort, my colleagues had voted to deny me tenure at Columbia University—my research on stock prices and taxes had just been too controversial.

Wearing a coat and scarf, I paused at the edge of the pond, reluctant to mar the smooth snow on top of the ice with my boots. Eventually, though, I stepped onto the ice and looked up, wondering where God had been during the crucial vote. Throughout my life, I had tried to place my faith in him. I felt he had led me to Columbia University in the first place and had encouraged me in my research. Now it seemed the path he had led me down produced nothing but failure and loss. Why had he steered me down this barren trail? Why had he turned away when I needed him most?

I felt forsaken, so forsaken that it was hard to muster enough faith to even pray. When I finally did, I asked for guidance in my career. I waited for an answer, for direction, but none came. The air was still. This silence made me feel even more alone than before.

I considered trekking back up to the house, but the hill was steep and my strength was gone. Inertia fastened my boots to the snow. My thoughts turned to the cold air and the moonlight reflecting off the snow. Then, ever so delicately, a more fundamental answer came. It was an answer I had received before, one that had helped anchor me through previous losses in my life. The answer was simply this: God was there, he had heard my prayer, and he loved me.

Although this isn't the specific answer I sought that night, it's the answer we all need the most. God is the fundamental fact of our existence, the driver of all security, meaning, and purpose. Through him, we can ultimately climb back up when pain and opposition beset us. Without him, we remain fastened in despair.

Although many choose to ignore our need for God, the events of our day make this more difficult. We've entered an era of instability and uncertainty. Greed, dishonest financial reporting practices, and sudden takeovers consume entire companies, forcing thousands of employees from their jobs and professions. Like me, many are left to wonder what they should do in their careers. Furthermore, powerful earthquakes and crushing waves pound nations. Hurricanes and floods destroy lives. Wars are harder to define and to win. Terrorism threatens our peace at home, and ominous new diseases arise. Without a doubt, this is a day of shaking and turmoil, and the tremors are cracking many of our conventional foundations of peace and security.

Amid all this uncertainty, the foundation of Jesus Christ is the only secure anchor. Without the assurance that God exists and watches over us, our failures seem random, meaningless, and absolute. Our losses seem irreparable, and our calamities eventually overwhelm us with despair. With the assurance of Christ, we can stand firm in confidence that he will ultimately restore our losses more completely than we can even begin to comprehend. Courage and optimism will sustain us through the turbulent times, and joy will overwhelm the pain. Faith in Christ is the answer we all need the most.

However, as the need for Christ increases, so does skepticism in Christ. Popular novels and magazines portray Christ merely as an effective teacher, not as the literal Son of God. Popular secularism contends that faith in Christ is naive and narrow-minded. Courts ban Christ from our schools and celebrations, and nations ban the symbols of Christ. Europe has entered what many claim is a "post-Christian" era, and some say the United States is moving down the same path.

This growing skepticism can challenge our individual faith. One night, a student approached me as I finished teaching a class on taxation. I anticipated a question about my lecture.

"Do you believe in life after death?" he said.

Surprised, I asked what prompted the question.

He indicated that a family member had developed a serious illness. "Sometimes," he said, "I wonder if men have simply invented God to fulfill their desire for immortality."

Such questions of faith are common, especially when life takes unexpected turns we don't understand. Just as I felt alone when I walked down to the pond behind my home, so we all feel forsaken from time to time, and we wonder if God is really there for us. To some degree, therefore, I felt as if I understood my student's concern. In fact, as he spoke I began to reflect back on a time when I had pondered a similar question in high school, wondering if there really is life after death.

The question pounded me one day as I was working on homework during a free period at school. I'm not sure what prompted the question; it seemed to hit me out of the blue. Once it did, it riveted my attention. As I saw it, there were two alternatives. If there's life after death, then the effects of even our simplest actions endure forever, and each friendship we forge initiates an eternal relationship. On the other hand, if there's no life after death, then the effects of even our greatest actions endure for but a moment, and each friend we lose descends forever beyond our view.

The prospect of this eternal separation and darkness weighed heavily upon me. I couldn't shake the feeling that man may have invented God to mask the darkness. Over ensuing weeks and months I engaged in an intense struggle to determine if God is really there. As a budding social scientist, I didn't want to be deluded by false hopes. I tried to address the question logically, but there were too many unknowns. I couldn't figure out the answer. The longer I remained in doubt, the more desperate I became. I feared I might be holding onto a terrible secret—God is a mirage and we are alone.

During this turmoil, I took a walk to the hills behind my home late one night. Hundreds of homes now cover those hills in Valencia, California, but in my youth they were largely undeveloped. I pulled up the top wire of the fence at the crest of the first hill and carefully squeezed between the barbs. Slowly, I then proceeded toward the rim of a small valley. I descended the forty or fifty yards to the bottom and knelt. I looked up, paused, and then began to speak, simply to ask if there was really anyone there to listen.

I don't remember how long I waited for an answer that night, perhaps hours. Then the answer wasn't what I expected. Instead of tangible evidence that God is real, a comforting peace settled over me. The peace didn't erase all my fears and doubts. It did, however, bear gentle witness that God was there, he had heard my prayer, and he loved me.

When I returned home that night, I felt torn. On one hand, I was disappointed I hadn't seen a tangible sign that God exists. On the other hand, I couldn't deny the fact that I felt more at ease. To further test the answer I had received, I returned to the hills many times after that. Over the following months and years, the original answer sank deeper and deeper into my heart. Ever so gradually, it softened my concerns, and I began to trust in it.

Looking back, I see the evidence I trusted came from within. Science typically rejects this type of internal evidence. In our age of reason, spiritual vision is deemed inferior to physical vision. A few years ago I sat down with a leading research scholar who held this view as he struggled with the lack of external evidence for the existence of God. "My wife passed away two years ago," he told me, "so I want to believe there's life beyond the grave. But I've concluded that there is just no way to verify God empirically."

Given my own doubts and questions as a youth, his statement had a familiar ring. Through my own search, however, I'd learned that the sure evidence of Christ is not only in external data, but is in the peace and assurance he bestows upon us as he whispers to our hearts. Even though we may be accustomed to trusting physical evidence alone, this internal confirmation is forceful evidence regarding the existence of God. If we are, in fact, eternal beings, then in regard to matters of eternity, it's our spiritual vision that can see through the transitory world in which we live to the enduring world beyond. In other words, spiritual vision is the sure link to our eternal identity.

If we embrace this internal vision, it fills us with impressions and insights that enlighten all we see in the external world. Through this vision, we begin to appreciate that God grants reflections of Christ unto us each day—ordinary images with extraordinary meaning. Gently, these images testify that Christ is real and that he is intimately involved in our lives. They impart meaning to our existence, and they provide evidence of Christ.

Often we see these reflections in the eyes and faces of others. When my youngest son, Joshua, was born, I held him in my arms and asked him the same question I've asked my other newborn children. "So, little one, tell me, what was it like to come from God's arms to mine?" Of course, Joshua didn't say a lot at the time.

A few weeks later, I felt he began to answer the question. He did so as my wife, Kristin, held him over her shoulder so he was facing the wall behind her. Kristin saw he was smiling away with a full-mouth grin. He was a sober child who hadn't smiled like that before. Curious, Kristin wondered why he was smiling so much. She adjusted him a little to see if he would continue to smile. He did. And for the first time in his life, he laughed. Really curious now, Kristin turned around to discover she was standing directly in front of a large portrait of the Savior. She had seen the reflection of Christ in Joshua's eyes.

I also remember seeing the reflection of Christ soon after my oldest son, Sean, was born. When he was just two days old, the nurse brought him into the room because he was crying. Unable to console him, the nurse handed him to me. I held Sean tight and whispered in his ear, "It's okay, Sean, Daddy's here." To my surprise, he stopped crying immediately and settled into a peaceful sleep. As he did, I reflected on Christ's words that we have a loving Father in the eternal worlds—a Father who is there to wrap us in his arms and share that love with us.

As we begin to see these simple reflections of Christ, they illuminate our understanding. This ability to see the world in a new, more complete light confirms our faith, providing tangible evidence that our original trust in spiritual vision pays off—it sharpens our eyesight. Rather than simply seeing a baby laugh or a newborn child settle into a peaceful sleep, we see and feel a witness of God's eternal love for us.

As we adopt this new perspective, we begin to forge a new personal paradigm—a new set of assumptions and premises we use to view and interpret life. In science, a faulty paradigm leads to puzzling and contradictory inferences from data. It's like trying to interpret the data through a distorted lens. When researchers discover a new, more correct paradigm, they can make sense out of their scientific observations, overcoming the confusion and apparent contradictions.

Likewise, when we adopt the paradigm of Christ and trust our spiritual vision, it helps us make sense out of our personal observations, as well as our challenges and difficulties. Through this paradigm, internal impressions and feelings regarding the unseen world, which may have seemed at odds with the external world, now help us see and understand that external world more clearly. Indeed, these internal impressions become the core substance of the more encompassing reality we now perceive. We begin to see meaning and purpose in all the events of our lives, including our failures and losses, which may have simply seemed confusing and contradictory before. We develop confidence that these losses can eventually yield eternal compensation. We begin to recognize deeper meaning in the commonplace events of life, and we find that these new insights are richly satisfying.

As we place our faith in this paradigm of Christ, we also appreciate the more profound reflections of Christ that God places along our paths, such as the image of those whom he transforms through his grace. While attending church one day, I saw this reflection in the face of a young single mother. As a result of tough circumstances, poor decisions, and some real mistakes, she had felt far from God. Speaking through an interpreter, she testified of God's cleansing, redeeming power, concluding, "Through Christ, I've come a long way in the last couple years, haven't I?"

Like the woman who washed Christ's feet with her tears, this young mother had come unto Christ, and Christ had healed her so completely that she now radiated deep joy. This evidence of a transformed soul far transcended any physical evidence I had ever seen in my academic research projects. The transformation was too complete to occur through willpower alone. Christ was in the change.

As Christ transforms us, he instills in us the genuine concern for others and the desire to serve and sacrifice without regard for worldly praise or reward. This sacrifice for others is itself a reflection of Christ. Christ didn't hold a high position in the world. He didn't graduate from a top university in Jerusalem. Nor did he hold a powerful title in business, education, or politics. Instead of following the path of popularity, comfort, and ease, Christ meekly labored among the most humble of people. Rather than growing up in affluence, he grew up in a dusty, poor village. His colleagues were simple fishermen. When he performed a miracle he didn't use it to promote himself. Rather, he often instructed witnesses to "tell no man." He healed the sick and blessed those who came to him in grief.

There are many ways to reflect this humble service, including parenthood. Indeed, the parallels between Christ's commitment to us and a faithful parent's commitment to a child are striking. In place of worldly prominence and prestige, parenthood often consists of difficult, quiet service to humble children. There's little prestige in waking up in the middle of the night to feed a crying baby or to calm a troubled child—there is no one around to applaud or to grant a promotion. Yet Christ was there to calm the troubled sea for his frightened disciples. Nursing a sick child back to health doesn't provide worldly prestige and honor, but it emulates the loving, healing touch of the Savior. Just as Moses esteemed the words of Christ to be of greater worth than all the treasures of Egypt, so parenthood places Jesus Christ and his example above the glory and honor of the world.

This type of self sacrifice abounds and is often overlooked. Nevertheless, it follows the pattern set by Christ. It defies the powerful natural impulse to protect and promote ourselves, supplanting it with the divine impulse to help and bless others. It reflects the best within us, Christ himself, who made the ultimate sacrifice for us all. Through self sacrifice, parents reflect Christ for their children to see.

In return, children sometimes reflect Christ for their parents to see. During the Christmas season, I saw this reflection when approximately 150 young people from several different religious denominations in our community gathered together to sing "O Holy Night." Bucking secular trends, these youth boldly sang out for Christ. After they sang, many of them commented on the deeply spiritual nature of the song. Others expressed feeling Christ as they sang.

The event provided compelling evidence of Christ. Despite the rise of secularism, despite the assaults on the name of Christ that sometimes make belief in him unpopular, despite the competing temptations of youth, and despite the two thousand years that have elapsed since Christ's day, these young people stood up and, through song, bore firm witness of Christ. If Christ were merely an effective teacher, he couldn't evoke such enduring praise. This was a witness of the literal Son of God.

These young people reflected the image of Christ because the Light of Christ is deep within each of them. This same light is deep within each of us as well, and it's in this light that we can find ourselves. Over the years, I've thought a great deal about this concept of finding one's self. It was a very popular quest when I was growing up in Hollywood during the 1960s and early 1970s. As a youth, I remember seeing many around me trying to find themselves in drugs, sex, loud music, and long road trips in brightly painted VW vans. As immortalized in a popular song of the era, others sought to find themselves by simply kicking down the cobblestones and feeling groovy. But when we turn to the Lord, our vision rises above the cobblestones we may be kicking down, and we begin to see we really find ourselves in Christ.

We find ourselves in Christ because Christ is the true light within us. This Light of Christ is the deepest, most genuine element of our being—nothing we can produce on our own begins to compare to the glory and majesty of the Light of the Almighty God who is within us. In a way, therefore, we're all connected to each other; the deepest, most sacred part of you is the deepest, most sacred part of me, and in both cases that part is Christ. This is one reason we're naturally drawn to the image and words of Christ—he is already part of us. When we see him, we recognize our true selves. In his light, we see our own reflection more plainly.

When we see the reflection of Christ around us, we also see the reflection of the eternal light within us. If we nourish this light, we step toward our true identity, understanding ourselves more clearly and expanding our vision. As we continue to submit ourselves to Christ, the love of God swells from within, increasing our capacity to love others. This expanded vision and increased capacity to love is the irrefutable evidence of Christ. When we experience it, we know it comes from God. As Christ transforms us, we become the evidence of Christ. We no longer have to guess whether God reigns in the heavens above—he reigns in our hearts.

Indeed, the ultimate evidence of Christ is not in what we observe, but in what we become as we journey to know him. This is the journey to know the deepest, best element of ourselves. We often encounter pain and failure along the way. Temptation may lure us off the path, and the burdens of pride and worldly ambition may weigh us down. However, as we learn to lay this baggage aside and cast our burdens upon the Lord, our vision and love expands and we begin to feel more joy as we climb.

Ultimately, the journey leads us back to our eternal home. When it does, we may be tired and tattered, but we have this promise: Christ will stand at the door to meet us as we arrive. He will know our name. He will sup with us, and he will seem familiar to us as we more fully recognize that he has been in us all along. At that time, we will no longer see his reflection in glimpses, but we will see him face to face, and we will find our home in him.

However, before that day of bright revelation we are still left to wind our way down dark trails to small ponds to pour out our hearts to the Lord. As we do, we may not always receive specific answers to the questions we pose, but if we listen carefully we will receive a deeper answer—Christ is in the eternity overhead; Christ is in the eyes and faces of our young children; Christ is in the tears and joy of those whom he transforms; and Christ is deep within our hearts. God is there, he hears our prayers, and he loves us.

two

TABERNACLE OF ETERNITY

The Light of Christ is woven deep into the fabric of our souls.

On Tuesday nights, it's my job to roll the garbage cans out to the road. The homes on my street are well spaced, and there are no street lights. In the darkness it's easy to see deep into the night sky—no artificial light dims the view.

On one particular Tuesday the sky was exceptionally clear. With thousands of stars over head as I looked up, I felt as if I were gazing into eternity. While I paused to reflect on the view, a bright star shot across the sky, trailing a streak of light. It emerged from eternity and returned to eternity in an instant, disappearing from view.

It was an ordinary shooting star, but it confirmed the impression we've all felt from time to time—like the star, we too belong to eternity. For a brief moment we emerge from eternity here upon the earth, springing forth from God, our eternal home. Then in an instant we die and disappear from view, returning to that eternity from whence we came, returning to our home.

At times, we all yearn for this eternity. Something inside whispers that we're not completely at home in mortality, with its boundaries, limits, deadlines, and death. It feels awkward. Innately we sometimes feel there is an enduring place of peace and meaning beyond our view—a being in whom our deepest desires may be fulfilled.

I remember one particular occasion in which I yearned for this eternal home. I was sixteen at the time, traveling with six or seven friends. My friends had just won a basketball tournament in Los Angeles and were headed to Oakland for the sixteen-team Western Final Tournament. I went along with them to provide moral support.

The tournament was held in a gym next to a towering white tabernacle, which caught my attention as soon as we pulled into the parking lot. I'd never seen a building like it before. My friends went on to win the tournament, prevailing in four straight games. However, my most vivid memory from the trip is the lone walk I took outside during one of the games.

Following a prompting from within, I left the gym and circled the tabernacle. Finding a private place in back, I reached out and placed my hands on the outside walls. As I did, my heart ached deeply to go inside. I wanted to walk through the locked doors to feel the wisdom and peace of that sacred building. That is, I wanted to step closer to God, my eternal home.

Although the cares of the world may bury this yearning to step closer to God, it's common to all. It is an integral part of our beings, springing from within. Indeed, the whispers that beckoned me to the tabernacle were the voice of God, spoken through his Holy Spirit. Just as Christ often said, "Come unto me" as he walked upon the earth, so he often whispers, "Come unto me" within our hearts.

These words spring from within because God has placed a slice of eternity within us. When we were born, we were all richly endowed with this eternal inheritance—the Light of Christ is woven deeply into the fabric of our souls. This same light gives life to all creation. It fills the expanse of eternity, encompassing the mysteries and riches of the entire universe. It's the ultimate source of all joy and fulfillment. By weaving his light into our souls, therefore, Christ implanted a kernel of the night sky within us, with all of its wonders and glories. When we look up and see a shooting star streak across the sky, we catch a glimpse of the eternal home that is embedded in us.

Although the eternity within us is as profound as the universe itself, God has laid out a simple, straightforward path to unlock its secrets. We have but to repent from our sins, place our trust in the light, and turn to Christ. If we do, we will feel his comfort and know his peace, being born of him. Through the voice of the Spirit, we will know God is there, even in our days of loss and despair. The Spirit will whisper that God hears our prayers and he loves us. He will testify that we have deep eternal worth as the sons and daughters of God, filled with the inheritance of Christ. He will also open our eyes to see the reflection and inheritance of Christ in others as well. Gradually, the Spirit will lift our vision above the counterfeit gold of this world to the eternal weight of glory in Christ.

Despite the straightforward path that leads to this joy and fulfillment, the artificial light of this world often dims our view. Lust, ambition, anger, and pride all call out to us more loudly than the Spirit speaks. We hear these calls so often that we may even forget the whispers of the Spirit are there. We may spend all our efforts seeking our fortune on earth rather than seeking our treasure in heaven, trading our eternal inheritance for a meager bowl of pottage from the world.

As a business professor, I'm only too familiar with this concept of seeking worldly fortune. When I teach MBA students or train stock market analysts, I focus on maximizing shareholder wealth, which makes sense to most of my students because we're all taught that more is better than less. In truth, however, more is only better than less if the assets we seek are real and if the cost of obtaining those assets isn't too high. Financially, nothing could be worse than squandering a rich inheritance in pursuit of false assets.

While sitting in a vacation rental home at Martha's Vineyard one day, I picked up some local tourist guides and learned a little more about this idea of squandering a rich inheritance for an imaginary treasure. I discovered that settlers first came to the island in the late 1500s and early 1600s. One prominent settler was named Thomas Hunt. At the end of one of his stays on the island, Hunt kidnapped a few of the natives and took them back to England as slaves. This group of kidnapped natives included an individual named Epinow.

Epinow quickly learned to speak English, but he yearned for his home, so he began to try to figure out a way to get back to Martha's Vineyard. After watching the habits of his captors for a while, he devised a plan. In particular, he began to hint that there were vast amounts of gold on the island, and that he could show his captors where to find it.

Inflamed by greed, Sir Fernando Gorges dug into his inheritance to finance a large ship, and Captain Hobson took Epinow and his crew to Martha's Vineyard to search for the gold. Epinow helped guide the ship to the southern part of the island, and when he saw his chance he jumped ship and swam to shore.

Captain Hobson and his crew scoured the island for the promised gold, only to discover that there really wasn't any gold after all. Epinow had just taken them for a ride. Epinow had fostered and encouraged the crew's ambition for wealth, power, and fame, but in the end the crew went away empty-handed.

Likewise, if we spend too much effort pursuing the treasures of this world, we will eventually come away empty-handed. Of course, we may find some nuggets of fool's gold along the way—fancy homes, power and authority, fame and popularity, or consuming lust. But in the end, we will find ourselves feeling hungry, unfulfilled, and dissatisfied in the famine that follows our day of squandered wealth, having traded the eternity within us for a counterfeit return.

On the other hand, if we step back from the pursuits of the world, even for brief moments, we discover that treasures of more enduring value are close at hand. Again on Martha's Vineyard, I once stumbled upon such a treasure. I had been walking down Circuit Avenue on the north side of the island. It was night, and the street was bustling with activity. The Flying Horses Merry-Go-Round was packed with teenagers trying to grab the brass ring that promised a free ride. Lines had formed at the Island Theatre to see the latest thriller movie, and shoppers packed into the stores. Nightclubs blasted their music onto the street.

It was exciting, and I was getting into the mood of this rather riotous scene when I came to an alley that led behind the street.

Curious, I walked down the alley to find a quiet, open place of worship surrounded by a circle of small, well-kept homes.

As it turns out, I'd discovered the Campground Meeting Place, which the local residents refer to as an outdoor tabernacle. Preachers held many large revivals here, especially in the 1800s. The peace of this tabernacle contrasted so starkly with the noise of the world on Circuit Avenue that all my senses relaxed and I felt a step closer to God. In this tabernacle, I felt the deep eternal inheritance within me, not the shallow transitory value of the world.

I later learned I wasn't the first to recognize the contrast between Circuit Avenue and the outdoor tabernacle. At one point those who attended the revivals built a seven-foot wall around the campground to separate themselves from the worldliness of the street. That way, participants couldn't sit at the back of the tabernacle congregation with one eye on the preacher and the other eye on Circuit Avenue. No fence-sitting was allowed. Each individual had to choose whether to focus on God or the world. If they chose to follow God they had to sacrifice the world, essentially placing their worldly desires on the altar of God.

We all have access to campgrounds of peace like this, sacred tabernacles that are close at hand. It could be the ponds or hills behind our homes, the churches where we worship the Lord, or the rooms where we pray. When we resort to these tabernacles, Christ strengthens and refreshes us. He comforts us, lifting the burden of our worldly cares. He infuses us with insight that takes us a step closer to him—the ultimate tabernacle of peace within our hearts.

Not long after I discovered the outdoor tabernacle on Martha's Vineyard, I stood in front of my family's old home on Old Norwalk Road in New Canaan, Connecticut. Built in 1901, this small, white home was full of character. We'd spent many years improving and decorating it. We loved the place, but when our family outgrew it we reluctantly moved. However, we were not reluctant to leave Old Norwalk Road. Our rolling acre of land with its stream, bridge, arbor, and garden was located on what may be one of the busiest and loudest single-lane roads in all of Connecticut. There were many summer days in which any attempt to take a shovel and enjoy working in the garden was interrupted by huge trucks barreling down the road just thirty feet away.

One particular day was different. Instead of holding a garden shovel, I held a snow shovel. Snow has a wonderful capacity to muffle the noise of the street. The few cars that drove down Old Norwalk Road that day passed without notice. It was quiet, so quiet in fact that I stopped to listen. The contrast was striking. Instead of motorcycles, trucks, and sirens, the only sound I heard was the steady, light tapping of snow falling on my jacket.

As I listened, I discovered the snow did more than just blanket the sounds of the street—it also quieted the anxieties of my heart. Before I stepped out into the snow I had been working hard to prove my value to the world. I'd spent the morning carefully crafting a report on my latest economics research, anxious to publish the study in a prestigious journal, hoping to earn the resulting security, honor, and financial reward. I had reached out to grab the audible, visible prizes of life—the gold of this world.

But now it was different. The falling snow melted away the competitive ambitions of my heart. For a moment, there was no thought of publishing my work in the most prestigious journals. No sounds of promotions, honors, or year-end bonuses. No call for success, prestige, or wealth. No shouts for stellar performance at work, at school, or on the stage. There was just the falling snow.

As my ambitions faded, the voice of the Spirit became clearer. I didn't hear of achievements or power, only of security. Instead of bid and asking prices on Wall Street, I heard peace. Regardless of the successes and failures of life—the demands, the frustrations, the pressures, the honors, the awards, and the embarrassments—I felt a place of deep intrinsic worth, freely granted to me, and to all of us, as an eternal inheritance: the love of the Savior. In comparison to this love, the wages of the world seemed dull and completely insignificant.

Christ is prepared to bestow this type of experience upon us all. In fact, when I've related the event to others, I've learned it isn't unique. Some say they've had similar experiences standing in the snow or walking in the woods, as they've stepped back from the ambitions, pressures, and stresses of life for brief moments of reflection.

It's not just coincidence that these impressions often occur when we're by ourselves in nature. Separated from the demands of society and the objects of worldly desire, we can listen more carefully to the voice within. Moreover, the Light of Christ that infuses us also infuses the natural world. When we take the time to step into the solitude of nature, its light kindles our light and we step into the companionship of Christ.

Moments like this seem to come and go like wispy clouds on autumn days. Once they evaporate, we may wonder if they were real. Springing from within as they do, the moments don't always leave any obvious external evidence to corroborate them. We may second guess the impressions and wonder if they were simply products of our imagination.

Nevertheless, if we trust the impressions enough to shed our worldly ambitions and let the Spirit work upon our hearts, the impressions will repeat themselves over time. Today we may catch a glimpse of the eternity within. Tomorrow we perceive the same truth, often with additional insight. The recurring nature of these impressions is itself evidence of their authenticity. It confirms that the original impressions were valid. Even more fundamentally, the impressions gradually change who we are. When they do, we eventually conclude that the moments in which we step aside from worldly lust to hunger for the presence of eternity are the most real moments of our lives.

Sometimes, though, the Lord sends more than just subtle impressions from the natural world to arouse us to the eternity within. Although the Light of Christ permeates nature and may fill us with insight, his light is especially strong in us, the sons and daughters of God. Often, it's in the common bond of Christ that we most clearly perceive our common eternal inheritance.

When I worked in Manhattan, an older Jamaican woman came to my office each morning to empty my trash can and sweep the floor. Whenever she came I never bothered to talk with her. I was too busy doing academic research, busy trying to exalt my career.

So we remained strangers. This went on for a few months until one day the Spirit whispered that I should reach out and get to know her.

I don't remember the exact question I used to break the ice. But I remember it beginning the first of many conversations. We began to talk with each other every morning. As we talked, I learned she was filled with courage, warmth, and love. She had raised several children of her own and was also raising three grandchildren, working hard during the day to support them financially and then spending hours with them at night. She faced trials and obstacles constantly, but she did so with optimism. She asked me details regarding each of my children and remembered those details without fail.

Before long, I found she uplifted and cheered me every time she entered my room. She reflected Christ for me to see, and I felt his light in her presence. At first I thought the Spirit had led me to set aside my worldly ambitions to serve her, but in the end it was she who served me. The Spirit had guided me to find the reflection of eternity within her, and in that reflection I feel as if I caught a glimpse of the eternal inheritance within me as well.

If we're perceptive, we'll discover that God grants each of us opportunities like this to find ourselves in the common bond of Christ. It may be a humble, kind friend who inspires us to live a little higher than we've lived before, a little further above the clamor of the world and a little closer to the eternity within. It may be a loving family we know whose example softens our hearts so we can feel the gentle tugs of the Spirit invite us unto

Christ. It may be a child who awakens our desire to live more purely. It may even be the custodian who empties our trash can and sweeps our floor. Whoever it may be, the common bond of Christ we feel in their presence is real. If we embrace this bond, it will draw us closer to the source of all true security and peace—Jesus Christ.

This is the security and peace I yearned for when I placed my hands upon the wall of the tabernacle in Oakland so long ago. It's the same peace we all yearn for. Like me, many have discovered traces of it while looking up at the night sky or standing in the snow. And beyond nature, they've yearned for it as they've placed their hands upon walls of tabernacles, temples, churches, and cathedrals—walls that express our common desire to find the eternity within us.

Thousands of miles from the tabernacle in Oakland, one such wall stands in the Old City of Jerusalem, a wall on which Christ himself likely placed his hands. Known as the Western Wall, it dates back to the Temple of Herod in Christ's time. Although it's only a retaining wall for Temple Mount and isn't really part of the original temple itself, it's as close to the original temple as faithful Jewish worshipers can get. On a day when I was there, many worshippers had gathered together, placing their hands on the wall as they prayed.

As I considered these faithful worshippers, the parallel between their quest and mine struck me. Just as I longed to step closer to God as I placed my hands on the wall of the tabernacle in Oakland, so they longed to step closer to the Holy of Holies—the heart of their ancient temple—as they placed their hands on the wall of Temple Mount. As I watched them, our mutual yearning for God became tangible. Their yearning stirred my yearning, and I found myself reliving my own ardent desire to step closer to eternity.

This shared yearning for God would have been enough to mark that day in my memory, but there was more. Just to the side of the wall is a path that ascends to the top of Temple Mount. After observing the worshippers at the wall for some time, I climbed this path. As I did, the visible horizon expanded with each step. At the base of the path all I could see was the wall and those who surrounded it. At the top of the path I looked out to see the entire Old City of Jerusalem to the north and to the west. To the south I saw the hills and valleys that lead down to the Dead Sea, and to the east I saw Gethsemane and the Mount of Olives. Leaving the world down below and walking up this Mountain of the Lord revealed new perspectives and insights, and I felt a little closer to home.

Likewise, as we step out of the mire and temptations of this world and begin to ascend the Mount of the Lord unto the tabernacle of eternity that is within our hearts, we will find the true Holy of Holies—Jesus Christ himself. No matter how far we may have strayed from him over time, we will learn he has always been there on the lookout, waiting for us to return. When we do return, through humility and sincere repentance, he will be there to bestow our eternal inheritances upon us—he will embrace us with his love, scrub our scarlet sins until they are white as snow, and lift us up to a higher vantage point to show us a deeper vision.

DEEN KEMSLEY

28

With Christ, we will begin to see beyond the horizon of this life into the riches of eternity, where he dwells. In his light, the gold of this world will lose its luster, becoming dull and dead unto us. In its place, Christ will fill us from within with his love. As he does, we will no longer have to look up at shooting stars to catch fleeting glimpses of eternity, for the morning star of Christ himself will arise in our hearts. He will transform us from within, placing his robe of righteousness and forgiveness upon our shoulders, his ring of eternal inheritance upon our finger, and his shoes of worthiness and peace upon our feet, as he lifts us up to become one with him, our true eternal home.

three

WAVES OF TRIBULATION

Christ's power to heal is deeper than our deepest pain.

$\mathcal{I}$ was sitting at the edge of the ocean, watching the waves sweep the sand over my legs and feet. As a three-year-old boy I was timid at first, but I edged closer to the water as my confidence grew. Without warning, an extraordinarily large wave hit the beach, dragging me into the surf.

I was completely helpless in the surge. It battered me against the ocean floor and pulled me farther away from shore. My mother and grandmother saw the wave pull me under, but when they ran to the water's edge there wasn't anything to see—I was lost in the waves.

I have very few memories from my early childhood. But I remember seeing sand and water rush by me within the dark waves. I couldn't breathe. I gasped for air. At that critical moment, an onlooker caught a glimpse of me and reached deep into the waves to pull me out.

My rescuer was a middle-aged man with a red swimming suit and dark chest hair. As I coughed and sputtered, he carried me back to my mother. He left before we had a chance to thank him. Since that day, I've thought about him often. I don't know his name, and he probably doesn't remember me. But I've always felt a close bond with him.

For me, this was a very personal encounter with the power of the sea. But in a way it's an experience we all share. Although the waves of the Pacific batter few, waves of disappointment, loneliness, and grief batter us all. Temptation may also overpower us and drag us into despair. There are times when the waves may overwhelm us for so long it seems we can't possibly hold our breath any longer. We can get lost in the tribulation and feel utterly alone—it's dark, and the pain can be so great it's the only thing we can sense.

When submerged in waters of tribulation, hard questions may come to mind. Why must we face this sorrow and pain? How could a loving God let this happen to us? When asking these questions, we're actually seeking much more than reasoned answers. We're seeking comfort and relief. Although explanations may help, what we really seek is love. Love from friends, love from family, and, in the end, love from the ultimate source of comfort: Jesus Christ.

We don't seek this love from Christ in vain, for he is ever ready to offer it unto us. In fact, if we could see more clearly, we would perceive that he is standing there next to us in the surf, waiting to reach into the waves and pull us up into his arms, where his power to heal is deeper than our deepest pain.

Christ perfected this healing power through sacrifice. Rather than standing on the sidelines and simply describing the need for pain and opposition, Christ descended into an eternal pit of affliction himself. He knelt in the garden of grief at Gethsemane and hung on the cross of sorrow at Calvary. When we face pain, therefore, we're not alone. Through his eternal grief, Christ developed perfect empathy. He knows our sorrow; he understands our pain; he cares about our loss; and through the power of his perfect empathy and love, he stands ready to take our burdens upon him. In a very real way, Christ feels all our infirmities.

The sacrifice of Christ was all-encompassing. He held nothing back. He yielded to the betrayal of a close friend, a disciple whom he had loved and served. He submitted to false accusations in the palace of the high priest, where he should have been revered as the Great High Priest. He subjected himself to the threats and ridicule of Caiaphas, who should have knelt to worship him rather than stand to sentence him. He gave way to the stripes of a brutal whip and to a crown of thorns.

Humbly, Christ then bore his cross as he started the arduous march to Calvary. Once there, soldiers transfixed him to the posts, driving nails through his hands and feet. They then lifted him up as his enemies reviled against him, wagging their heads, taunting him, and mocking him. Here Christ suffered inestimable pain, pain that we can't begin to fathom. And as he did, he took our sins upon him, finishing his work of salvation for men.

Before he subjected himself to the physical pain of the cross, Christ submitted to the spiritual pain of Gethsemane. Descending into the pit of Kidron, he knelt at the base of the Mount of Olives. He was alone. Even Peter, James, and John, his beloved disciples, had fallen asleep. Sinking deeper into the pit of despair and pain than anyone else has ever gone, he took our sorrow upon him with pain so great that he sweat great drops of blood.

The depth of this eternal sacrifice testifies of the depth of Christ's love for us. This love is very personal. As the omniscient eternal God of heaven and earth, Christ sees and understands every sin we commit, every inadequacy we feel, and every sorrow we bear. He knows exactly why his suffering was so great. Christ not only suffered for the world as a whole—he also suffered specifically for you and for me. Given the personal nature of this sacrifice, he feels a deep personal bond of love and concern for each of us.

Through this personal bond, Christ can sustain us through our grief and loss. Sometimes he manifests his power unto us in our daily routines at home and at work, where disappointment often abounds. At more dire times, he bestows his peace upon us when we face deep trials, finding ourselves in the very jaws of sorrow and tribulation. Through the power of his resurrection, he also provides the hope and comfort we need so dearly when we must stand at the doors of death. Finally, he grants his redeeming grace upon us each time we sorrow for our sins and call upon him.

In regard to Christ's power in our daily routines, I recall one hot summer afternoon when I was sitting in my office at the university. One of my MBA students appeared at the door. "I studied just as hard as I could for the midterm and still failed," she said anxiously. "I don't think there is any chance for me to pass the final."

It's not uncommon to hear such statements during office hours. In response, I simply talked through the subject matter with her. We continued in this manner for a few minutes, focusing on accounting principles. Suddenly, a sense of empathy arose in my heart. Caught off guard, I paused to ponder. My thoughts turned to Christ and the understanding and concern he must feel for this troubled student. At that moment, the student began to relax. The experience enabled me to catch a small glimpse of the profound personal nature of Christ's compassion and healing power.

Many years earlier, I had felt a similar impression, only more deeply. It occurred while sitting down to eat lunch with coworkers at a Vietnamese restaurant in San Francisco. A couple of my associates were Vietnamese and had helped me order from the menu as they reminisced about their early years in their native country.

"My father had been killed, so my mother was alone," said one of them as she began to tell her story. "My mother felt the 'soldiers' would come after us next so she told my older sister and me to leave. I tried to get my mother to come with us, but she said my little brother and sister were too small to go. She would have to stay back with them."

There were four or five of us leaning over the table to hear her account. She spoke matter-of-factly, not emotionally. She was thirteen years old when she had to flee. Her sister was fifteen. "My mother hoped the little ones were so small the men would ignore them, but she said it was too dangerous for me to stay."

Like many who fled Vietnam and Cambodia in the 1970s, this young woman and her sister had to escape through the jungle on unmarked paths. Their mother gave them some money, and they headed for the coast, traveling at night. When they arrived, they paid a fare to a boat owner who promised to ferry them across the Gulf of Siam. But when they approached the dock the next night, they discovered a band of soldiers. The boat owner had betrayed them. Slipping into the trees, they walked two more days through the jungle, moving farther down the coast. This time they secured passage.

The boat was very crowded, and when my friend and her fellow passengers were only a day or two out from land the motor failed and they began to drift. One day they were excited to see a large speedboat coming their way. They waved and cheered to draw attention. However, when the boat pulled up beside them the men pulled out guns, robbed the refugees, and left. A couple of days later, another boat arrived. They didn't wave or cheer this time. When the men on this boat discovered the passengers had already been robbed, they were angry and started hitting some of the passengers.

After being attacked twice, the refugees started to rip wood planks off the deck floor to use as oars. It worked. After two or three days of rowing they came to shore. No one on board was exactly sure where they had landed, and there was no one on land to greet them. Day after day, they remained alone, living off the fruit they found in the trees. Without shelter, they endured heavy rains.

"After the rain stopped each afternoon, I laid out on a rock above the sea to dry out my clothes," she continued. It took more than a month for someone to discover the refugees. At that time they learned they had landed on the southern peninsula of Thailand.

My friend and her sister spent two years in a Thai refugee camp before being shipped off to California, where they were separated. "My foster family was very nice, but I couldn't speak the language and I felt terribly alone. Each afternoon after school I climbed down into a pit alongside the road to cry for an hour or so before returning to the house."

It was easy to feel compassion for her as she spoke. Insurgents had killed her father. She had to flee her home, leaving her family and friends behind. Someone she trusted had betrayed her. She had endured hunger, thirst, fear, and fatigue. Pirates had attacked her on the open sea. She was exposed to torrential downpours, and in the end she found herself in a foreign land she didn't understand. Bereft of all she knew, she had lost much.

However, her words elicited more than simple compassion. As she spoke, it was possible to catch a glimpse of Christ's sacrifice in her pain. Her suffering made Christ's suffering feel a little more tangible and real. It helped me feel closer to him, a little more grateful for the depth of the sacrifice he endured for us.

Her inner confidence was also impressive. Instead of expressing resentment, she conveyed hope. Since Christ is the ultimate foundation for all genuine confidence and hope, it was evident that Christ had begun to heal her. Seeing the power of his redeeming grace begin to restore her strengthened me. It was a visible witness that Christ's power to heal is, indeed, deeper than our deepest pain. If we submit to him, then ever so gradually he will carefully wash away our pain and sorrow through the power of his infinite Atonement, replacing our grief with his love, one fiber of our souls at a time.

This relief from grief is among the most profound blessings of God. Each time we experience it, it is precious. This may be especially true when we face the ultimate loss of life—the loss we must all endure in the end: death itself. By hanging on the cross and rising from the tomb, Christ purchased the power to wash away the sorrow of death just as entirely as he can wash away all the other sorrows of our lives.

Over the years, I've seen this power in the eyes of many men and women who faced death with courage and faith, trusting that God would be there to greet them in the land beyond the veil. However, it was my wife, Kristin, who saw it a bit more dramatically one day as she stepped into the hospital room of an older woman, a friend named Marjorie.

Marjorie was a close friend of our entire family. She lived on a small farm just down the hill from our home in Connecticut. My boys and I would often go down to her farm to see the animals. Marjorie always greeted us with a smile. It was a smile we grew to treasure, and it was a smile I got to see one last time when I too visited her in the hospital. But it was Kristin's visit that stood out.

As Kristin entered the hospital room, Marjorie didn't respond. She was too sick to even perceive that Kristin was there. Kristin sat down beside her and began to rub her hand. Marjorie didn't react at first, but gradually she began to awake.

"Happy, happy, happy," she said.

Sensing that Marjorie might have caught a glimpse of the world beyond, Kristin then leaned over and asked, "So have you seen your loved ones in the next world?"

Marjorie then said, "Oh yes, warm, happy, happy, happy."

That was to be Marjorie's final testimony here upon the earth, a testimony with meaning for us all. Even though death can be unbearably difficult for those who remain behind, Marjorie's words bore witness of the deep comfort that can await each of us when our turn comes to pass through the veil. Through Christ, our death can be filled with great joy.

Sometimes, though, Christ's redeeming love fulfills an even more sacred role. Rather than cleansing us from the sorrow imposed upon us through failure, oppression, betrayal, or even death, there are times when it must wash away the ultimate anguish—the heartache of sin. Sin causes the most profound pain because it separates us from God, severing our ties to the source of our most profound joy. Many of us know the overshadowing darkness and hopelessness of sin, the feeling that we have let ourselves and the heavens down, the feeling of anxiety regarding the justice of God.

One fall day, I gained new appreciation for this anxiety regarding ultimate justice. My daughter and I were on our way to visit friends when we rounded a curve and came face to face with a motorcycle. The eighteen-year-old rider slammed his bike into the front left corner of our car. My daughter and I were not injured, but the motorcyclist was in a great deal of pain. He was bloodied and had what appeared could be a broken limb or two.

Despite his injuries, the young man seemed reluctant to have me call for help. Nevertheless, I dialed 911. An ambulance soon arrived, accompanied by the police. After the paramedics bandaged him up, the police turned him over onto his stomach, cuffed his hands behind his back, and locked him into one of their cars. Seeing my surprise, one of the police officers explained there was an outstanding warrant for the young man's arrest. At a moment of great pain, justice caught up with him.

I shuddered a little at the strict demands of this justice. This young man had past crimes. I have past sins; all of us do. Given these sins, strict justice implies there should be outstanding warrants for my arrest in the heavens, and for each of us. In fact, each time pride, lust, or selfish ambition enters our hearts, we create new offenses for review at the judgment bar of God. Seeing officers place handcuffs on this young man's wrists in his moment of pain brought me close—too close—to the exacting demands of justice.

This feeling of anxiety regarding sin isn't imaginary. The justice of God is real and strict. Indeed, to maintain the integrity of the kingdom of heaven, this justice must be perfectly strict—any pride or selfishness in that place would compromise the sanctity of God's kingdom and render it unclean. Given this anxiety, there are times in which each of us longs for redemption, a way to place those sins behind us and move forward in hope.

This desire for redemption is so deeply ingrained in our souls that it permeates the customs and beliefs of societies all around the world. One night many years ago, I was surprised to find it deep in the jungles of Southeast Asia. In November of 1976, I visited Lopburi, Thailand, where I joined a large procession walking down to the river. Passing the Buddhist temple, I crossed the bridge and worked my way slowly through the throng to the far side of the river. I had been in the area for a while and recognized some faces in the crowd. But I had not seen so many of them together in one place before. It seemed as if the entire town had gathered to celebrate the annual Loy Kratong festival.

Under a clear sky, the light of the stars and the full moon reflected off the water in front of me. The river was small, and the setting was modest—small wooden shacks lined the shore. But the excitement was intense. Everyone was waiting to float, or *loy*, their kratongs down the river.

Each kratong consisted of a small wooden boat about eight inches long. Banana leaves and bright pink and yellow flower petals formed the sides. Candles stood in the center. As it grew darker, anticipation for the launch rose. As the excitement grew, I began to ask around, "Why do you loy kratongs down the river?" There were many answers, but one impressed me. "We place our grief and sins on the kratongs and send them down the river to wash them away and to bless us with peace and happiness." I've since learned that according to Thai tradition it's the light from the candles that carries away sin.

The launch then began and thousands of candled kratongs filled the river. The water literally became a river of light. The light was so bright it seemed to illuminate the sky. It's hard to describe the feelings I experienced as I watched the light flow down the river. I had come to the river feeling lonely, but as I beheld the light of these living waters, serenity reigned. I stood transfixed. Fulness replaced emptiness. Harmony replaced loneliness.

The lighted kratongs that night provided clear evidence of the inborn desire for redemption. In retrospect, I find it interesting that many of the individuals who stood along the river that night hadn't even heard of Jesus Christ. They didn't know he is the true light of the world, the source of living waters, and the only one with real power to carry away our pain and sins. They also didn't know how dearly Christ had sacrificed for them. Innately, however, they desired everything his sacrifice provides—peace, joy, and atonement from their sins.

When we face the strict demands of justice and are filled with this desire for redemption, Christ's sacrifice becomes especially dear to us. In these moments, we realize how valuable it is for us to have him take our handcuffs upon him. If we place our trust in him, he will answer the demands of all our outstanding warrants. He will reach deep into the waves of sin to pull us up into living waters of light, where he will wash us clean from even our darkest stains. If we submit fully to his tender cleansing care, the comfort and relief will be absolute and will bind us to him in eternal gratitude.

Nowhere can we feel this bond more fully than when we immerse ourselves in the living waters of Christ and let him wash us clean from our pain and sin. Christ has promised that when he returns to the earth he will cause a river of such waters to spring forth from his throne on Temple Mount at Jerusalem and flow down to the Dead Sea, with waters deep enough to swim in. Everything this river touches shall live, and trees of life shall line both banks. The fruit from these trees shall fill those who partake of it, and the leaves shall heal those who handle them. The river will then heal the Dead Sea completely, bringing it back to life.

Nevertheless, we don't have to wait for Christ to return to the earth for us to step into the river of light and life he has prepared for us. This river is primed to flow in our hearts now. Through his sacrifice, Christ has placed the tap for an eternal spring of living waters within each of us. Indeed, the Light of Christ himself is woven deep into the fabric of our souls.

Just as Christ has power to heal the Dead Sea, so he has power to heal us completely. Furthermore, he has an eternal vested interest in us. If we stray into the waves of sin, he will not stray from us. He will sweep every nook and corner of our hearts to find us, and he will wade into the surf to catch a glimpse of us, calling upon us to return to him. If we respond to this call and place our trust in him, he will then pull us up into his arms in an infinite embrace where the joy of eternity will wash away even our deepest pain.

four

ALTAR OF GOD

*If we place our will upon the altar of God, he will
lead us to find our deepest, truest selves. No self-devised
detours lead to this end.*

My father held on to my hand as we climbed the rugged path together. It was covered with yellow-brown shale—loose rock that broke apart when we stepped on it. We'd received a strict warning to avoid this slippery, dangerous shale. We proceeded slowly, trying to avoid as much of the shale as possible.

Early in the climb we came to a steep ravine, about eight feet deep and ten feet across. Shale covered both sides. It was essentially impossible to cross without touching much of the forbidden shale. When we reached the far side, the shale became less dense. With renewed effort, we tried to avoid the shale as we continued to climb. My father helped me, lifting me over rough spots and pointing out shale as we went.

This hike through the mountains seemed very real to me when my father told me about it in February of 1961, a few days before I turned four years old. In reality, it was just a dream. Since I'd tagged along with him in the dream, I listened closely to my father's words, wishing I could have seen the dream as well.

In the dream, my father and I eventually reached the crest of the hill, where we could see others forging ahead along the same path. They were making good progress, but we could see that the shale along the path grew thicker and thicker. The only trail that appeared to be relatively free from shale led down to our left. It was narrow, dusty, and covered in sagebrush. From all appearances, it wasn't promising.

As we stood at this fork in the road, I looked completely to my father for direction. After peering down both roads as far as he could, to where they bent into the sagebrush, he took the low dusty trail. He hoped it would help us find another way up the hill with less shale than the first.

After taking this turn, we proceeded to the bottom of the dusty trail. My father stopped to look back at our path. As he did, he saw others walk by without hesitation, keeping to the main road that was covered in shale. My father's heart ached for them, but he didn't know why—they were moving quickly, and the path my father had chosen had produced nothing but sand and sagebrush. Nonetheless, he was concerned for them.

Slowly, my father then turned back to the dusty trail and continued down the path. After traveling down the trail for some time, the sagebrush eventually gave way to a small park with a circular patio. Stone benches sat around the circumference of the patio and a raised fish pond stood in the middle. Looking beyond the pond, he saw a large hotel. Intrigued by the hotel, my father proceeded toward it. As he did, armed guards emerged at the gate.

At first we were frightened by the guards, so we hid behind the raised pond. Eventually, however, we stepped out and approached the guards, relieved to see they meant no harm. When we reached them, the guards engaged us in friendly conversation, but they wouldn't let us pass through the gate. At that point, we noticed one of the guards was holding a small box. Sensing the box contained passes into the hotel, we asked for the silver tickets he held. He smiled, reached into the box, and produced a silver ticket for each of us.

My father then lost sight of me as he turned to enter one of the elevators in the lobby of the hotel. After he ascended a few flights, the doors of the elevator opened to what he described as the most beautiful sight of his life. The room he beheld was filled with light and was entirely done in silver except for a six-foot red velvet border along the edge of the floor. A huge crystal ball hung over the center of the room, filling the room with reflections of light. His mother and father were there, and everyone seemed extremely happy.

My father was just about to step out into this room when the elevator operator closed the doors, promising that there were other rooms for him to see. That's when my father woke up. I've always wished he could have slept a little longer to see where the elevator went next. After taking the long trip over a rugged mountain trail and a dusty desert path, he caught but a momentary glimpse of the hidden treasure at the end of the path—a beautiful room filled with reflections of light.

Over the years, I've thought a great deal about this journey through the hills, even though it was simply a dream. As in the dream, there have been many times my father has held my hand and showed me the way. Nevertheless, the dream takes on its deepest meaning for me when I consider the hand we can all reach up and hold as we walk the rugged paths set before us, a sure hand that will never fail—the hand of our Savior, Jesus Christ.

Just as Christ is there to pull us out of the dark waves of pain and grief when they overwhelm us, he's there to reach down and help us over the rough spots of life, pointing out the dangers of temptation and sin as we go—the shale upon the earth. In most cases, he will not altogether lift us out of our trials. Life is meant to be a challenge, a test to determine if we will have the faith to cast our cares on the Savior. At times, we may find ourselves standing in deep ravines covered in temptation, hardship, and pain. Nevertheless, Christ is there to strengthen our steps through rugged terrain. If we look to him completely for direction, he'll become our sure guide down the path of discipleship that leads us back to him.

Compared to the path of the world, the path of discipleship may seem low and dusty. It isn't nearly as popular to follow the path of Christ as it is to follow the path of sin. Unlike the path of sin, the path of Christ doesn't promise the lust, pleasures, and riches of the world. However, if we trust and believe in Christ enough to let him take us down this path, he will eventually lift us up to a beautiful illuminated kingdom filled with reflections of his light. This is the only path leading to the deepest, best part of ourselves—the only path where we can find our true selves. All of eternity lies at the end of this path.

However, the path of discipleship requires sacrifice—sacrifice of our worldly lusts and ambitions, as well as all other things the Lord requires. This sacrifice is central to the purpose of life. It has always been a prominent feature of the trail. From the days of Adam and his righteous son Abel to the day Jesus Christ sacrificed his life for us, God has called on men to build altars and offer sacrifices of the firstlings of their flocks, their best gifts, unto him.

Even now, God expects us to sacrifice as we walk down the path of discipleship. Of course, we may disregard this call. When our desires clash with the Lord's desires, we can choose our will over his. Given this agency to choose as we please, the determination to follow God is much more than simply a decision to comply with mandates imposed upon us. When we obey, we're actually placing tokens of our own will upon the altar of God as gifts to him. These tokens are often small. But they are meaningful to the Lord. He receives them with joy. It helps perfect our bond with him.

If we offer such tokens and choose to stay upon the path of discipleship, taking Christ as our guide, he will continue to call upon us to offer new sacrifices unto him. In fact, each of us will receive our own unique set of opportunities to offer sacrifice. Often, though, the calls are for rather ordinary sacrifices of time and effort to serve others. Although these plain offerings are not as dramatic as our momentous sacrifices, they form the bedrock of the path.

Simple sacrifices of time and effort abound. I felt the effects of one such sacrifice when three of my MBA students came to me separately to tell me about one of their classmates. In each case I heard reports like, "He spent hours helping me get ready for the exam," "I couldn't have made it through the course without him," and "He's an excellent teacher."

The reports surprised me. MBA programs are competitive, and for this course the students knew the school prescribed the number of As I could assign. The only way to get an A was to push another student down to a B, and I knew all of these students would eventually compete for the same jobs. Despite the intense competition, this particular student was willing to set aside time and personal ambition to tutor others without compensation. The report impressed me. It was more memorable than the exams I graded. It was a small but real token of sacrifice.

One reason this report impressed me is that when I was in college I often focused more on the success of my own studies than on the success of others. Later, when I was a young father working as an accountant, I continued to focus on the success of my work, often at the expense of time for my family.

At the time, my wife and I had four children and she often needed my help. However, I usually left for work before sunrise and didn't come home until after dark. At that point I would try to help out, cleaning dishes or reading bedtime stories, but my heart wasn't always in it. Often the demands at work occupied my heart and mind. I couldn't begin to imagine ever having more than four children—I already felt stretched to the limit.

This type of focus and concentration is fairly normal among young parents trying to establish careers. Nevertheless, self-sacrifice—not self-promotion—marks the path of discipleship. Eventually, the Lord found a way to help turn my heart toward others. He did so through my wife and family, and through my own desire to go back to school for a PhD.

I'm not sure exactly why I wanted to go back to school. I was progressing toward partnership with the firm, and I knew it would take at least four years to complete the PhD. Understandably, my wife, Kristin, was reluctant for me to leave my job to become a full-time student. However, one day she came to me with a proposal. "Deen," she said, "I'll support you in your desire to go back to school if you'll support me in my desire." As she spoke, I thought of the bachelor's degree I knew she wanted to complete. She caught me completely off guard when she said, "I would like to have two more children."

I thought hard about the proposal. It would be difficult enough to get through the PhD program with four children—six seemed impossible. In the end, though, I agreed, and we moved to North Carolina for four years of school.

As the family grew, my heart changed. With six children I found it impossible to protect my old life and ambitions any longer, so somewhere along the way I threw in the towel and embraced the new life I was living. I took more joy in the children. Eventually, I reached the point where I even felt excited when my wife announced the impending arrival of child number nine.

My family helped me place some of my own plans for life upon the altar of God. God replaced those plans with a much richer, more meaningful life than I'd planned for myself. Moreover, in this new life I began to discover a deeper, better part of myself, a part that felt sincere joy in others, a part that felt a step closer to Christ.

Of course, sometimes the plans God asks us to sacrifice run deeper, cutting to the core of our hearts. When these requests to sacrifice the treasures of our hearts come, they are seldom welcome. They can be confusing and often seem to make little sense, and they can be deeply painful. Nevertheless, the calls come from God, who descended deeper into the pit of despair and pain than any of us have ever gone and who loves us more dearly than we can understand.

Thousands of years ago, it was Abraham who received such a call. Abraham and his wife Sarai had pleaded unto the Lord for a child, but the plea seemed to go unheard. Year after year, they remained without child, but they persisted in faith. Finally, in their old age, God gave Abraham and Sarai a child. They named the boy Isaac.

After some time, the Lord came to Abraham with an exceptional request. He asked Abraham to take his son to Mount Moriah and sacrifice him upon the altar of God. No one knows exactly what thoughts went through Abraham's mind that day. But the request couldn't have made sense to him. God had promised Abraham that he would multiply his seed as the stars of the sky and as the sand of the sea. Yet God was asking him to give back his son, the son through whom the promise would be fulfilled.

Abraham didn't hesitate. Early the next morning, he saddled his ass, took his son, and started up the dusty path of discipleship toward Mount Moriah, which is now Temple Mount. At the base of the mount, he took Isaac by the hand and climbed the path to the top, where he built an altar. Then he placed Isaac on the wood and stones and took the knife to slay his son. At that moment, the Lord sent his angel to spare Isaac, but not until Abraham had proved he would hold nothing back from God, that he valued his bond with God above all things.

Through this sacrifice, Abraham found the deepest, best part of himself. The Spirit of the Lord swelled within him, filling him with knowledge, understanding, and love. Jehovah and Abraham became close, so close in fact that God adopted Abraham as a "friend," welding an eternal bond. God then bestowed an eternal inheritance upon Abraham, blessing him eternally in the heavens and multiplying his seed on the earth until he became a father of many nations. Abraham had proved he was willing to sacrifice his old life and his own desires upon the altar of God. In return, God lifted Abraham's cares off his shoulders and bestowed a glorious new life upon him.

Although we are not tested exactly like Abraham, God asks each of us to sacrifice desires or objects that are dear to us. For me, the sacrifice of my academic position at Columbia University stands out. After being voted down for tenure, it was hard for me to let go of the position. In fact, it was so difficult that on one dark night I stepped out of the house to find a private place where I could ask the Lord to perform a miracle on my behalf. Although it was unprecedented, I wanted to ask him to overturn the tenure vote.

When it came time to speak, however, I surprised myself. I wanted to ask for a miracle, but instead I simply said, "Father, if it be thy will, I offer my career unto thee." Somehow I felt Christ wanted me to make this offering instead. The Spirit whispered that he who had knelt at the altar of Gethsemane and offered the ulti-mate and free-willed sacrifice, saying, "Not my will, but thine, be done," would receive joy in my small offering to him.

After making this offer once, it was easier to make it again. I repeated the words of the prayer. If God wanted me to leave my career behind, I would. Instead of trying to battle back as planned, I'd move on.

Despite the words I spoke, part of me hoped the Lord would turn down the offer. I still wanted a miracle. Looking back, though,

I think he took me for my word. The research career is now largely gone. Nevertheless, just as Christ granted a richer, deeper, more meaningful life unto me as my family grew, I believe he has granted a richer, deeper, more meaningful life unto me since the night I spoke these words. I now have more time to focus on my students and to really get to know them. I have more time to focus on my family and to enjoy them. I also seem to have more time to reflect on the sacrifice of Jesus Christ and on his deep love for us.

Although this career sacrifice seemed meaningful to me at the time, there are deeper treasures to sacrifice than our careers. At the same time I lost my job, a close friend of mine lost his job as well. But that wasn't his greatest concern, for he also lost his beloved wife. She had battled cancer just as hard as she could, but in the end she passed away.

My friend was then left to raise the children on his own. Her death just didn't make any sense to him—or to any of the rest of us. His pain was deep. He wondered why God had called him to suffer this loss, and there were no easy answers. Like many before, he wrestled with the heavens, seeking help and meaning.

It's not possible to fully understand this type of sacrifice from the outside—the loss is profound. I tried to support him, but I felt largely helpless. It seemed that all I could do was observe. I noticed that he began to submit to the Lord, offering his will upon the altar of God. Just as Christ humbly submitted to death as he hung on the cross, saying, "Father, into thy hands I commend my spirit," so my friend essentially said, "Father, into thy hands I commend my dear wife." He turned his loss over to Christ, whose power to heal is deeper than our deepest pain.

Christ didn't lift him out of his trials, but gradually Christ began to strengthen his steps and to bring comfort and solace to his heart, supporting his growing efforts to continue on with his life. This cleansing process isn't complete, for there is much to heal. However, his bond with Christ is deeper than before. When I talk to him now, I can feel the power of Christ within him. Through this growing power, he strengthens me.

As we offer these humble gifts of faith to Christ, ultimately we begin to see that what Christ is really asking us to do is to offer our whole souls unto him, submitting to him entirely in complete trust. We make this offering to him one small step at a time, a sacrifice here and a sacrifice there. But in the end, only an absolute offering will do. Recall that when Christ called Peter, James, and John to be his disciples, they left their fishing nets behind and forsook all to follow him. Later, Christ made it clear that if we're to be his disciples, we must follow the example set by Abraham—we must hold nothing back from the Lord.

From our mortal perspective, this can be viewed as tough doctrine. It requires us to believe in Christ no matter what. God understands it's hard. If we're not willing to make the sacrifice, God gives us the option to turn aside from the path of discipleship at any time, going just as far as we choose. However, the path ends in one place, and one place alone: Jesus Christ. To reach that end, we must submit everything unto him.

This type of submission requires deep faith. It requires us to give up that which we see, feel, and cherish as a gift unto the Lord, whom we do not see. It requires us to trade a visible treasure for an invisible return. Yet this return is the ultimate promise of eternity. It includes the covenant that we will be born again as God transforms us into new creatures in Christ, rooting out the man of sin. He will fill us from within with knowledge, understanding, and love that reaches to the heavens, and he will lead us to find our deepest, truest potential. No self-devised detours lead to this end.

On one occasion, I feel as if I saw a brief preview of this promised return, although only faintly. My wife and I were flying back from a short trip to New Orleans. I dozed off and began to dream. In the fleeting dream, I saw a partially-raised curtain that was transparent enough for me to catch a glimpse of a beautiful light-filled room behind it. As I looked at this room I thought it must be the kingdom of heaven. I wanted to enter. But almost immediately, I began to think of reasons why I might not be worthy to enter. My past sins and mistakes discouraged me. After a moment, though, my outlook changed as I remembered the sacrifice of Jesus Christ. At that point, I began to cry out in my dream, saying, "I call upon the Atonement of Christ to wash me clean so I can enter the kingdom." My feelings were so poignant at that moment that I woke up.

In retrospect, I see that when I stood before the curtain of this light-filled room, I had no thoughts regarding the treasures I'd lost during life. Career failures meant nothing. The payoffs of the world just didn't matter in that place, and all my sacrifices seemed small and insignificant. For a fleeting moment, my vision was clear, and the only thing that did matter was whether or not I would be admitted into the kingdom. The glory of that room far transcended the cost of my sacrifices—so far, in fact, that the cost seemed trivial.

Nevertheless, our sacrifices are not trivial to God. They are deeply meaningful to him. He receives each small gift of faith with joy, amplifying it within the bosom of eternity. If we're steadfast upon the path of discipleship and let the Savior raise us all the way back to him, we'll eventually kneel before the true altar of God that stands before his throne in the heavens. Christ will there reach out to embrace us in the joy he feels. At that time, we will know the pain of sacrifice and loss no more, but will be filled with the joy of his infinite sacrifice for us—the joy of eternal love.

five

PATH OF SIMPLICITY

*T*he homemade basketball hoop behind my house didn't look like much. My father had used a 4-inch by 6-inch piece of lumber for the post and an old wood pallet for the backboard. It was sturdy, though, and strong enough to withstand heavy use. As a boy, I spent a couple hours a day shooting hoops against that old board.

When I grew a little older, my father would take me to see the Los Angeles Lakers play on their home court. I felt a thrill every time I stepped into the building. As a teenage boy, it felt as if I were stepping onto holy ground. Someday, I hoped, I'd play on that court.

As an eighth grader, my dream of becoming a star on the court seemed within reach. I dominated the games my friends and I played during lunch and recess, towering over my opponents. I looked forward to playing each day, relishing my success on the court.

In ninth grade, my world changed. I stopped growing, but my friends did not. Gradually, I lost my edge. I tried out for the freshman basketball team, confident I'd be able to play. I made the team but was devastated to learn the coach had placed me on the fourth string, far back from the starters. I never touched the ball in a game.

As a sophomore, I battled back, struggling with all of my might to earn a spot on the court. Although I still spent the bulk of my time on the bench, the coach put me into some of the last few games of the season. This chance to play encouraged me. During the off season, I worked hard to prepare for the next year.

As a junior, my persistence paid off—the coach gave me the starting position as point guard for the junior varsity team. I was thrilled for the chance to bring the ball down the court and set up the plays. In one of the early games that season, I scored ten points, my best ever. I still remember hitting a sixteen-foot shot from the corner of the key. My team won its first seven games, and my dream of becoming a star on the court began to simmer again.

At that point, we lost two or three games, and I thought I was losing my edge. The coach then informed me that he was replacing me in the starting lineup. He promised that I would be the sixth man, the first one to come in off the bench. But as the season wore on, I played less and less.

The last game of the season was against Canyon High School, our arch rival. We controlled the game from the opening tip-off, taking a large lead. Eager to play, I sat on the edge of my chair waiting for the call. It didn't come as soon as I expected. Eventually I sat back, resigned to wait until after halftime. In the second half, we extended our lead and the coach began to empty the bench. One by one, my bench mates stepped onto the court. They played hard while I looked on. Finally, with a minute and a half left in the game, the coach called me in. I touched the ball briefly two times and the game was over.

That was the night I realized my dream was over as well. I would never star in the NBA. I would not even start on a varsity high school basketball team. The bus ride back to my home school was unbearable. I bottled my emotions, waiting for a chance to release them in solitude. I've never forgotten the pain of that night.

Having failed in my efforts to star on the court, I left Los Angeles as soon as school was out that summer and drove north to work on a small farm. At first this new venture was discouraging as well. My allergies were so severe that I wheezed and struggled for air whenever I exerted myself. I thought I might have to quit and go home. After two weeks, however, the allergies suddenly vanished, and I settled in.

I worked alone, moving sprinkler pipes and bucking hay. There was no one there to compare myself to, no way to star on the court or to get stuck on the bench. Although it was exhausting, it was a simple job without any way to do anything spectacular. But in this simple setting, something meaningful happened. I began to treasure the still moments under the open sky with the clouds, the hills, and the breeze. Far from the noise of the gym, I began to hear a new voice, a voice too still to hear on the court back home. It spoke through gentle impressions. Rather than fostering a desire to perform before eager crowds, it quietly testified that I could stop striving so hard—simply moving sprinkler pipes and bucking hay was enough for now.

I wondered if it could really be that simple. I wondered if I could really fulfill the deeper purposes of life without great, visible accomplishments. But as I listened to the voice within, it lifted a burden off my shoulders, testifying that there is a time to strive and a time to stop striving. At that period in my life, it was time to stop striving so hard and simply do the straightforward tasks at hand.

Peace and assurance accompanied this counsel, encouraging me to trust and follow it. As I did, the peace increased and I trusted it more. By summer's end I felt closer to Christ. In this simple setting, I had a more meaningful experience than I could ever have had on the basketball court.

Fortunately, the voice of God isn't confined to small farms under open skies. If we listen, we can all find this voice within us, a voice that will place us on the specific path of purpose and meaning the Lord has prepared for each of us. As we walk down this path, we'll find it's largely paved in simplicity. At times, God may call on us to perform great feats—difficult tasks that require all of our faith and might to fulfill. Often, however, he'll call on us to perform simple tasks. From these acts, he can transform our small offerings into eternal deeds that we could never accomplish on our own.

Long ago, the Lord taught this lesson to Naaman the Assyrian. Naaman was a powerful general who commanded armies and made great conquests. But when he contracted leprosy, the prophet Elisha instructed his servant to tell Naaman to simply dip himself in the River Jordan seven times to be healed. At first Naaman balked, believing he was worthy of greater, more notable deeds and upset that Elisha would not see him personally. Upon persuasion, however, he humbled himself enough to perform the simple act. God then healed Naaman, washing his leprosy clean.

Once Naaman decided to immerse himself in the waters of Jordan, it was simple for him to proceed. His real hurdle was finding the faith to trust in such a simple task. So it is with us. It's easy to visualize the benefits of great, visible deeds. It may require faith for us to believe we can accomplish them. Exercising this faith takes us closer to God. However, it often doesn't require faith to trust in the fruit great deeds will bear; we can see the fruit from the beginning. On the other hand, it's difficult to see the benefit of the simple acts God prompts us to do. This requires trust in unseen fruit, a belief that Christ will recognize and honor our actions, even if nobody else will. That's precisely why Christ recognizes and honors simple acts of faith, magnifying them with power and imbuing them with enduring value. They may not elicit the praise of man, but they engender the appreciation of God, drawing us closer to him.

Furthermore, following the path of simplicity relieves us from the burden of working so hard to become a star on the courts of life. Long after the summer I felt the Spirit whisper that simple acts of faith are enough, this same voice spoke to me again—this time as I sat on a bench in a grove of trees in upstate New York.

My ill-fated tenure vote at Columbia University had driven me to the grove. Stunned by the defeat, I had to decide whether or not I should fight back against those who opposed my research. Weeks earlier I had looked to heaven and offered my research career unto the Lord. At this point, however, I didn't know if the Lord had accepted my offer. I wondered if what he really wanted me to do was to brave the challenge. To some degree, I hoped he did. If he did, I felt he would support me in the endeavor. I didn't want to give up my dream of academic stardom if I didn't have to.

Contrary to my inclinations, the following words arose in my heart as I sat in the grove: "You can stop striving so hard." At first I wondered if this was just a fleeting, random thought. It was not. Time after time, the voice within me repeated the same words. "You can stop striving so hard."

These six words represented the only clear guidance I received that day, but as I thought about them I felt they meant I didn't have to become a star in the world of research after all. It was enough to simply teach my students, love my friends, and invest more time in my family.

At first, I resisted this message because it required me to give up long-held desires. It took time to absorb the new direction and begin to internalize it. However, as I gradually accepted it, I felt relief. I began to realize what a heavy burden my quest for academic achievement had placed upon me—more pressure and stress than I'd recognized. As the burden lifted, I appreciated my new freedom to savor the simple joys of life—family, friends, good books, long walks, and new adventures.

Christ offers these simple joys to us all. Although life often requires us to strive with all of our might, the Savior promises that his yoke is easy and his burden is light. If we listen, there are junctures in each of our lives in which we can hear the same message I heard. "You can stop striving so hard." We can set aside the ambitions that are sapping the joy from our lives and trust in the reassuring promptings the Lord sends unto us, the inner voice that says it's okay to focus on some of the simpler joys and tasks at hand.

As for me, I especially enjoyed my new-found freedom to focus on family. One summer afternoon after a long day at a Nantucket Island beach, my children gathered together for activities and games in the shade of a backyard. The older children taught the young ones how to swing a bat, and they started a game. Tired from the beach, I just watched. Gratitude washed over me. At the time, I wasn't exactly sure why I felt so grateful. I just sat back and enjoyed it.

Looking back, I think part of the gratitude I felt was for the children themselves. I recognized more clearly how much I enjoyed their companionship, and I was grateful to be their father. Part of it, though, was gratitude for the rich harvest the Lord had produced from the simple acts of service my wife and I had performed in our home over the years. Changing fifty thousand diapers, reading seven or eight thousand bedtime stories, settling hundreds of squabbles, and waking to crying babies more than two thousand times never seemed easy—it was hard work. But these tasks were not great, visible accomplishments. Parents all around us were performing the same work. What I didn't anticipate was just how rich a harvest these actions would yield. I'm now awed by the power of these simple acts, grateful to our Redeemer for lifting the burden of academic achievement off my shoulders so I could enjoy my children more fully.

Of course, the world often derides the simple acts we perform within our homes and deems them as naught. On one occasion, a colleague at Yale University argued that investment in our children doesn't really pay off—they eventually just grow up and go away to college anyway. If we really want to make a lasting impact, he argued, we need to dedicate ourselves to an enduring institution. Of course, the institution he had in mind was Yale.

An interview I once read in *Newsweek* magazine echoed a similar sentiment, this time from an author who insisted parents should stop wasting expensive education degrees in the nursery. As she stated, having two or three children takes a parent out of the workforce for an average of thirteen years, and that's a shame because work in the world brings influence, honor, compensation, and a hand in shaping the world around us.

In truth, however, when we're performing small acts of service in our homes or among our friends, we're laying the foundation for a great, eternal work that far transcends the politics of our day, a work that Christ will amplify with his redeeming grace to yield eternal influence, honor, and compensation. Sending our children to college, watching them move out of our homes, or even facing death itself can't remove this compensation from us. The remuneration of God endures forever. No sincere, humble investment we make in our families or friends will ever be wasted.

I've often seen this enduring compensation in the homes of others. It exists wherever selfless sacrifice exists. One evening, for example, I discovered it when I took one of my daughters to a school friend's home to play.

Following my daughter's directions, we drove up to a humble home on a busy corner, a cottage in a town of mansions. As I approached the door, I wondered why my daughter had chosen this particular home to visit, a place that lacked the prestige of all that surrounded it. However, when I stepped over the threshold of the home, a feeling of comfort and respect swept over me. At first I didn't understand why. The inside of the home didn't look much different from the outside.

Then I met the mother of my daughter's friend—a woman who worked as a nurse at night and served her family devotedly throughout the day. Given her tough schedule and lack of sleep, I couldn't help but think I'd just become tired and cranky if I tried to do what she did. Yet she was filled with optimism and enthusiasm. Though her tasks were difficult, they were simple and unnoticed by the world. They were not unnoticed by God, however. He had magnified her efforts, sanctifying her home with his presence. Through simple acts, she fulfilled a faithful mission in life. She wasn't a star in the world, but she was something much higher—an instrument in the hands of God.

Likewise, each of us can fulfill the deeper purposes of life by performing the simple acts God would have us do. Christ himself set the example. Although filled with might and power, he spent his mortal ministry performing simple, yet deeply meaningful, acts of obedience, submitting himself unto the will of the Father in all things. He taught, he served, and he healed in the most humble of circumstances, personifying simplicity.

Christ loves our simple acts as well, not only because they follow in his footsteps but also because they amount to little on their own and can't be mistaken for extraordinary personal achievement. They only produce fruit as Christ magnifies them. When he does, the harvest he generates can dwarf our small contributions, leading us to marvel at the power of his hand in our lives, filling us with appreciation and drawing us closer to him. In other words, simple acts of faith leave ample room for the power of his redeeming grace. Unlike many remarkable deeds, simple deeds don't squeeze out the Savior with the burden of their own greatness.

Furthermore, it doesn't really matter what simple acts we perform as long as they are acts Christ would have us perform. I've spoken much of the simple acts of service we perform in our homes, but we draw closer to Christ every time we reach out to someone in friendship and love, obey God's counsel, or complete the small tasks he sets before us. Even moving sprinkler pipes and bucking hay yields eternal compensation if that's what God would have us do at the time.

Of all the simple acts we may perform, the simplest may be to just believe. It requires faith to believe we don't have to earn our way back to God through notable deeds, or that Christ loves our small, quiet acts of kindness and obedience. It requires faith to believe we don't have to build a tower of good works that reaches so high it touches the heavens before we can enter therein, but that Christ freely offers to lift us up to him from wherever we may be. It requires faith to believe we don't have to scourge ourselves in penance for our sins to be forgiven, but that Christ can take our stripes upon him, wash us clean, and fill in the holes we gouged through our own mistakes. If we simply trust in him and submit our will to his, that's exactly what he will do.

I now return to a gym at a high school. This gym is at New Canaan High School, and I was there to see my daughter's team play one of the last games of her senior year. Work in Manhattan had prevented me from seeing her other games, so I was especially happy to be there that day.

Following in my footsteps, my daughter hadn't played much during the season. When her team jumped out to an early lead, I sat on the edge of my chair, wondering if the coach would put her in. As he looked into the stands, I think the coach saw me and the remainder of our large family watching with anticipation. Eventually he put my daughter into the game.

Immediately, she went to work. She rebounded, passed, and brought the ball up the court. She set up plays, scored a layup, hit a sixteen-foot shot, and put in three free throws. Each time she scored, her teammates shouted for joy. They seemed even more eager for her to score than she was herself.

Near the end of the game, she set up from outside the three-point line and released the ball. Even though her team had a large lead, I could almost hear her teammates hold their breath as the ball hung in the air. When it came down through the net, her entire team stood up on the bench, jumped up and down, and cheered for her like they had never cheered before.

She hadn't started, but she had scored ten points for her varsity high school basketball team that day, her best ever.

On that day, I felt as if I had actually found part of my purpose in life on the basketball court after all. More precisely, I found myself in the little girl I had once held in my arms when she was young, the girl I had served and cherished throughout her life. The joy of seeing her teammates stand up to cheer and root for her was overwhelming. As I watched, I realized I had become a small instrument in God's hands in something that really mattered—not in becoming a star on the court, but in raising a daughter I loved.

This opportunity to become an instrument in the hands of God is there for us all. If we humbly follow Christ down the path of discipleship, he will magnify the small, faithful efforts of our lives, transforming them into moments of overwhelming joy. No longer seeking to star on the courts of life ourselves, we will find ourselves in the love of Christ. If we're steadfast, the days of feeling burdened by ambition will fade into the past as the voice of God eventually invites us to put off our shoes and step onto the most holy ground of all, the soil of the kingdom of heaven. On this sacred soil, Christ himself will welcome us into his house of eternity to feel the power of his redeeming grace forever more.

six

BOND OF GRATITUDE

To know God is to know joy, and when we're filled with gratitude we know that joy most completely.

It was dark in the small room—dark, that is, except for the night-light behind my brother's bed. I'd played hard outside all day, to the point that my lungs had begun to sting from the smog. Now I could feel the pain of every breath even more acutely than before. This pain didn't make sense to me. In the past, breathing always became easier when I stepped out of the haze back into the house, but tonight I was gasping for air.

Despite the quiet of the night, I'd awakened suddenly. When I first opened my eyes, the darkness seemed thicker than usual. Now it stung my eyes as well as my lungs. It was a familiar feeling—before the days of emission controls, dense smog often enveloped Los Angeles even more than it does today. However, I wasn't accustomed to sensing the smog here in my bedroom at night. Eventually, the darkness became so thick that it drove me from my bed out into the hall. Uneasily, I opened my parents' door and stood by their bed.

"It's too smoggy to sleep in my room," I declared. "Can I sleep in here with you?" Tired, my mother simply told me to go back to bed. Reluctantly, I obeyed and returned to my room, only to become even more convinced that the darkness there was too thick for me to sleep. With renewed resolve, I returned to my mother to say that there just was no way for me to sleep in that smoggy room.

Groggy, she climbed out of bed and led me by the hand back out into the hall. When she turned on the light she stopped. She saw smoke billowing out of my room. Fully awake now, she ran back into her bedroom to rouse my father, who had to crawl on the floor with a wet towel over his face to pull my younger brother Mark out of his bed, just as it burst into flames. I don't remember what happened next. Somehow my father must have put out the fire, which the nightlight had ignited. I do, however, remember feeling grateful to escape the smoke and flames.

Nonetheless, as a young boy I quickly put the incident out of my mind during ensuing days, refocusing on friends and sports. As far as I was concerned, the fire was a done deal. On the other hand, my mother wasn't so quick to forget. A few days later, she expressed her gratitude, testifying that she didn't believe I woke up on my own. In her mind, it was no accident. She believed God had saved my brother and me from the smoke and fire.

I think I would have forgotten my mother's words just as easily as I'd begun to forget the fire if it weren't for the clear impression I felt as she spoke that her words were true. Today, the fire is a vague memory. The impression from her words, though, is still vivid in my mind. With the impression comes a sense of deep gratitude— gratitude that God had reached down to save my brother and me from the fire, gratitude that God was there to care for us.

In effect, this feeling of gratitude sealed and perfected the incident for me. Without the gratitude, the experience was incomplete—there was just smoke and fire. With it, there was a meaningful encounter with the Lord, a moment that bound me a little closer to him. It was a sacred moment, a moment in which I began to understand that God is really there and he loves us. Even now, whenever I think back on my mother's words, the feeling of gratitude returns, and I begin to feel the depth of the Lord's love for us all. In these moments, he doesn't seem far away.

Just as gratitude sealed and perfected this experience for me, so it perfects all of our experiences with the Divine. Whether Christ saves us from physical or spiritual perils or whether he simply speaks peace to our hearts in seasons of grief, our gratitude for this relief acknowledges his hand in our lives and creates a mutual relationship that helps bind us to him. Without gratitude, our relationship with Christ is one-sided. He bestows his mercy and love upon us, but we don't reflect that love back to him. Like a mirror that's lost its luster, his light expires in us. On the other hand, if we open our hearts to gratitude we joy in the gifts he bestows upon us, and he joys in the appreciation we reflect back to him. This mutual joy binds us together in an eternal relationship. Indeed, to know God is to know joy, and when we're filled with gratitude we know that joy most completely.

A couple years after enduring the smoke and flames of my bedroom fire, I traveled to the Colorado River. The trip underscored the value of gratitude and a mutual relationship with Christ. My father and I joined friends boating on the river. After navigating up and down the river for a while, my father let me drive. As evening approached, the water receded, and one of the other boats in our party got stuck on a sandbar. My father needed to go help them so he dropped me off on a small island, along with my brother Mark and a somewhat older companion, promising to come back soon.

At first, my brother and I didn't mind being left behind. We had fun exploring the island and watching the boats pass by. But this fun wore off as soon as the boats all returned to the dock and when we found there was nothing left to explore. The island was no more than forty or fifty paces long in each direction. I began to feel trapped. After a while, I simply stepped to the edge of the water to wait for my father to return.

I stood for what seemed to be a very long time, always expecting him to appear but never finding his form on the water. When evening turned into night, I continued to stand at the water's edge, but still there was no sign of him. I began to wonder why my father hadn't returned as promised. Why had he forsaken me? By this time, the air had turned cold and my companions and I didn't have anything to keep us warm. We were hungry, and as the moon rose higher and higher into the sky we became sleepy.

Finally, we were so exhausted that my brother and I lay down on the ground to rest. But thorns, cacti, sharp rocks, and the cold made it difficult to sleep. I felt more miserable than I could remember. Discouragement and loneliness set in. I felt as if we'd been abandoned on the rock, forgotten and left to suffer alone. I longed for my father's return.

Sometime, very late in the night, I heard the sound of an approaching motor. When it drew near I saw it was a boat heading directly toward us. I didn't recognize the boat or any of the people on it, but my older companion seemed to know our rescuers well. They pulled up to the island and got out to help us onto the boat. When we were secure, they ferried us over to a campground on the far shore. As we rode they told me that my father had been stranded as well. He had run out of gas and was facing difficulties of his own.

Most of the people in the camp were asleep when we arrived, but a few men had stayed awake to welcome us. They had prepared a warm fire for us, and they placed a blanket over our shoulders. They then poured us bowls of hot soup, which we quickly downed. After I'd eaten, they gave me a comfortable sleeping bag and placed me on a soft, flat patch of ground, much better than the rocks and thorns of my island bed. My relief was absolute, filling me with comfort like I'd never known before. As I drifted off to sleep I felt a profound sense of gratitude—gratitude for the men who had left their camp to come rescue us, and gratitude for the hand of God, which I sensed had guided them to us.

That night on the Colorado River wasn't the last time I've felt abandoned, forgotten, and alone. At times, we all feel that way. There are occasions when each of us longs for a sense of belonging, for the feeling that we're standing on the inside rather than being stuck on the outside. There are periods when it's as if we're all stranded on a shore and are waiting for relief, hoping for someone to remember us, waiting for someone to rescue us. In one way or another, loneliness besets us all. And with this loneliness there often comes a profound hunger—hunger for meaningful companionship that can fulfill our deepest yearnings.

If we hunger for the companionship of the Lord during these times, we don't stand upon the shore in vain. Christ descended deeper into despair than any of us can possibly go. He stood upon a shore of infinite anguish, marked by a cross, where even he reached the point he felt so abandoned he cried out to his Father, saying, "Why hast thou forsaken me?" His loneliness was absolute.

Christ endured this loneliness and abandonment, which eventually led to the tomb, for us. When he emerged from the tomb, he was filled with empathy and love. With this love, he creates a place of deep intrinsic worth within our hearts, a campground of peace, a refuge to which he offers to ferry us. If we accept his offer, he warms us with the fire of his everlasting light and places his blanket of comfort on our shoulders. He gives us rest from our burdens, and he feeds our hunger for meaningful companionship with a deep eternal bond.

It's then through gratitude that we secure that bond with Christ. As we offer our gratitude unto Christ, he often blesses us with a deeper understanding of his sacrifice. To a small degree, it's then as if we've stepped into Gethsemane or stood upon Calvary to see the Savior's grief, loneliness, and pain, to feel the depth of his loving sacrifice for us. As we begin to understand the depth of his loneliness and pain, we comprehend that Christ understands our loneliness and pain as well. This fosters further gratitude and the desire to understand his sacrifice even more. Hence, our gratitude begets understanding of his sacrifice, and this understanding begets further gratitude. If we're faithful, this cycle of gratitude and understanding grows stronger and stronger until Christ eventually perfects the mutual bond between us and him.

While sitting in Yale Medical Center one evening, I detected a hint of this link between gratitude and understanding. A surgeon had just removed the tonsils from my sixteen-year-old daughter, Tamarra. She was supposed to go home that night, but the recovery was so painful that the doctor and nurses recommended that she stay in the hospital. As she lay in her bed, she tried to speak. From where I sat I couldn't understand what she was saying. I moved closer. "If this pain helps me understand the sacrifice of Christ even a little bit better, it's worth the pain a hundred times over," she said.

As I've thought about my daughter's words, it seems that her pain must have given her some new insight into Christ's sacrifice for her. With this understanding came gratitude, a growing appreciation for the loneliness and pain Christ had endured for her. With this gratitude came a desire for more understanding. In my daughter's moment of crisis, therefore, she wasn't alone. In a small but meaningful way, she was thinking of Christ and felt his presence and love for her. Through her gratitude, Christ strengthened her bond with him.

This type of gratitude is much more than a simple nicety or something we're supposed to feel. It's central to our relationship with Christ. Without it, our bond with him can never be complete. We may labor our entire lives to perform righteous works, but if we're not sincerely and deeply grateful for the sacrifice of Christ, our works will mean nothing when we stand before the judgment bar of God. Like the empty works of the Pharisees that Christ often condemned, any attempt to use these works as bargaining chips to earn our way into heaven will fail. Only through gratitude can we draw upon the power of Christ's sacrifice in our lives, and only gratitude guarantees that our righteous works are what they're supposed to be—humble gifts of love and obedience that we lay upon the altar of God. When we offer this type of gift unto Christ, it fills him with joy and helps bind us to him.

Nowhere do we have the opportunity to feel this bond of appreciation and gratitude more deeply than when we feel Christ's redeeming grace wash us clean from our sins. The burden of sin can be heavy, more depressing than any other load. With its weight, life can be gray and filled with despair. To some degree or another, we all know what it's like to walk through the valley of sin, to stagger through the dark mists of transgression. When we do, we begin to understand that there's no way for us to emerge from this darkness on our own. We are captives to misery, trapped on an island of our own making. In these times, there's one hope and one hope alone: Jesus Christ. Through Christ alone comes the promise that though our sins are as scarlet, they shall be as white as snow.

If we sincerely desire to repent and open our hearts to Christ's mercy during these times, his joy begins to replace the pain. As our trust in him grows, the joy increases. Eventually the joy overwhelms the pain. This feeling of forgiveness and joy is one of the most precious gifts of God. It's the ultimate miracle. It has power to fill us with heartfelt gratitude unto the Lord, drawing us closer to him.

Over the years, I've personally felt the joy of Christ's forgiving grace many times. There have also been many occasions in which others have met with me to testify of the utter relief and whole-hearted gratitude they've felt when Christ came to rescue them from the shores of sin. During these meetings, I've learned how destructive sin can be, tearing apart families and ruining relationships.

However, I've also seen the power of Christ's grace to overwhelm the effects of this sin. As these individuals have spoken, the Spirit drenched both them and me in the love of Christ, perhaps more than any other times in my life. The gratitude they felt for the forgiveness of Christ was as exquisite as the despair they had felt for the sin. These were moments in which I could actually see and feel Christ strengthen his bond with man.

Within this bond that Christ forms with us, he drives out all vestiges of loneliness. He infuses us with his light, filling us with his own heart and mind, transforming us from within. The light with which he transforms us is the same light that permeates all around us, so as we become one with his light we become one with others, thoroughly connected with them. No longer standing by ourselves or feeling stuck on the outside, his light ushers us to the inside, to the inner sanctum of all meaning, purpose, and love—the bosom of Christ.

In this sanctum, Christ will then sanctify the smoke, flames, and fiery afflictions of our lives, using them to weld an everlasting bond with him. Eventually, he will seal this bond with his greatest gift—eternal life. As described by John the Revelator, he will forge a beautiful sea of glass and fire for us—home for them whom Christ grants victory over death and sin, home for them whom Christ transfigures with his light. In this home, our campground of peace, our gratitude will know no bounds as Christ calls us up to become one with him in eternity.

seven

BRIDGE TO ETERNITY

Forgiveness complements and completes our submission
of all judgment unto Christ.

$\mathcal{I}$ stood as tall as I could upon the ancient stone wall, straining to see it wind its way through the rocks and hills. No matter how far I hiked along the crest of the wall, I couldn't find the end—the wall seemed to stretch on forever. It was tall and wide, more than four times my height and wide enough, they say, for eight horses to stand side by side.

As I stood, I tried to imagine the many northern tribes the wall had repelled in its past. For thousands of years the Chinese viewed their nation as the center of the world, the Middle Kingdom. They built the Great Wall to protect the Middle Kingdom from the barbarians on the outside. The wall was so tall and wide it helped repel China's enemies for hundreds of years, defending the kingdom from its foes.

However, the wall came at great cost. It took more than two thousand years to construct. The labor went on for generations. A man's sons, grandsons, and great-grandsons would lay stones on top of the stones the man himself had laid. The sun was often hot, the stones were large, and many perished under their heavy burdens. Some estimate that as many as a million of these early masons died under the weight of the stones, transforming the wall into a vast tombstone.

Beyond the grim costs of construction, the wall also isolated the empire from others. More than almost any other nation, China developed on its own. This isolation preserved the nation's traditions and cultural heritage, providing unmatched continuity from generation to generation. However, it also cut it off from the knowledge, richness, and opportunities that lay beyond its borders.

As I consider this massive ancient wall, I can't help but consider the wall we're all tempted to build for ourselves. Not a wall to protect us from true adversaries, but a counterfeit wall that doesn't protect us from any real enemy. I speak of the wall Christ condemned time and time again, the wall he rebuked more than any other sin. That is, I speak of the wall of unrighteous judgment—unrighteous judgment against others, against ourselves, and ultimately against God. Within this wall we eventually just become isolated and alone.

Like other great walls, the wall of judgment can make us feel as if we're at the center of the earth. It protects our view of the world and preserves our traditions, defying outside influences. It lifts our self image above our fellow man and strengthens our perceived power.

However, the wall of judgment comes at great cost. When we entrench ourselves behind it, we may spurn the rich new opportunities and frontiers the Lord places in our paths. Prejudice against people and places may prevent us from even exploring options that could expand our horizons and bind us to others. Opting to defend our own kingdoms, we fail to embrace the more meaningful life Christ would bestow upon us.

Many years ago, I discovered a wall of judgment in my own heart. While growing up in Los Angeles, I was an avid Dodger fan.

I was at Dodger Stadium with my father on the night Don Drysdale pitched his record-setting fifth shutout in a row. I listened to hundreds of games on the radio and scoured the sports pages each day for news about the team. But up in San Francisco, it was the Giants who played ball. Now as Californians know, Dodger fans and Giant fans don't mix well. In my case, I grew up with a strong, very wide wall of prejudice against San Francisco.

It's hard to describe how deep this prejudice ran in my heart. It was so deep that when I once went camping and saw a van with a San Francisco Giants' bumper sticker on it, it angered me. To this day, that bumper sticker and my resentment toward it are my only clear memories of that childhood vacation. In a sense, I viewed San Francisco as the capital city of the northern barbarian enemy.

Nevertheless, when I was twenty-nine years old, I made some career blunders that limited my options and essentially forced me to try interviewing for a job in San Francisco. The trip required me to set aside my prejudice. When I entered the city's financial district that day, the Spirit overwhelmed me with the confirmation that this was the place the Lord had prepared for me. I was surprised by the strength of the confirmation. Despite my deep personal biases, I couldn't deny it. Therefore, I swallowed hard, took the job, and moved my family to Petaluma, north of the city.

After moving to the San Francisco area, I still stayed away from Candlestick Park, where the Giants played ball. But each workday for almost five years I crossed over the Golden Gate Bridge into San Francisco. As I did, I saw windsurfers, sailboats, and the beautiful city in front of me. I began to feel as if the bridge were taking me to my own personal promised land of joy each time I crossed it, a rich frontier beyond my original wall of judgment. I learned to love my work there, to love the bridge, the city, and the people. No longer weighed down by prejudice, I had been freed from the burden of my pride.

Perhaps not surprisingly, I felt this joy where a wide wall of judgment had once existed in my heart. When we step outside our walls of contempt and cross bridges of reconciliation in their place, the Lord leads us down the path to him across what can be viewed as the bridge to eternity. He lifts our burdens, opens new frontiers before us, and fills us with joy, immersing us in the grace of Christ.

This joy can only be found outside the walls of judgment. If we stay behind such walls, they block off the new frontiers Christ would open unto us, trapping us in narrow fortresses of our own prejudice. Moreover, the walls cast dark shadows upon our perceptions, distorting our view of others and preventing us from seeing the Light of Christ in them. Blind to the Light of Christ and to the good in others, our walls of judgment isolate us from both God and man.

I still remember one of the first times this distorted vision beset me. It was during sixth grade at Arminta Street School in North Hollywood, California. My handwriting was so poor my teacher made me stay after school one day to work on it. I stewed and fretted, angry that he had detained me. When I finally went home, I told my mother about the injustice, declaring that my teacher was a mean man. After that, the slightest provocation from him reinforced my judgment that he was simply mean. I retained this wall of judgment between him and me throughout the school year.

During the summer break that followed, I received some somber news. My teacher had passed away, and I learned he'd been battling painful cancer throughout the year. I felt awkward and guilty for the feelings I had harbored against him. Given his pain, I now realized I'd been wearing blinders, acting without all the facts. My vision had been distorted, and my judgment had been unduly harsh. I regretted that I had walled myself off from him and that it was now too late to apologize.

I incurred this remorse because I trusted my distorted vision and sense of injustice more than I trusted the counsel of Christ to simply forgive and let go. The Savior is very direct on this point, saying that if we don't forgive men their trespasses, neither will our Father in Heaven forgive us. This is clear-cut doctrine. To pass over the bridge to Christ and to feel his cleansing joy in our lives, we must forgive others. There's no other way. We may perform good works ad infinitum, but if we fail to leave unrighteous judgment outside the gate of eternity, we will not cross. We can't become one with Christ with a grudge in our hearts.

This commandment to forgive is especially challenging if someone has inflicted a serious injury upon us. It could be a competitor who has destroyed our career, an employer who has abused us, a friend or spouse who has betrayed us, or a brother who has stolen from us. Whatever the offense may be, it takes both courage and faith to forgive if we've incurred deep loss. Knowing this, Christ holds out a promise of infinite mercy if we do. He promises that if we judge not we will be not judged. If we forgive men their trespasses, so our Heavenly Father will forgive us. Consider the depth of this mercy. Even if we struggle with sin, which we all do, we have

God's promise that he will forgive us—utterly and completely—if we forgive those who have offended us.

Forgiveness begets forgiveness in this manner because it's largely through forgiveness that we tap into the power of Christ's atoning sacrifice. When we forgive those who have offended us—those who have essentially stolen treasure from us—we surrender our claim of justice for that stolen treasure unto the Lord. It's a gift that indicates we love Christ so dearly we're willing to offer a cherished claim unto him. In response, Christ cherishes our relinquished claim, forgiving our every trespass and bestowing the treasures of eternity upon us.

Beyond these judgments we may impose on others, there's another facet to judgment, a facet that's often overlooked. Namely, it's to be careful not to judge ourselves too harshly. It's natural to judge ourselves because we all make mistakes and experience failure, sometimes more often than we succeed. We learn of new shortcomings and inadequacies constantly. We hear others disparage us, and we see others who seem superior to us. Sometimes, we also commit outright sin, often injuring others in the process. One way or another, it's easy to find evidence that we just don't measure up.

When we feel this way, Christ's command to judge not takes on new meaning, encouraging us to lift our eyes above the despair we feel to the eternal promise within us. It's a directive to judge ourselves in Christ's loving light rather than to judge ourselves in our own harsh light, trusting in the power of the Atonement.

As the parents of nine children, Kristin and I know the burden of self judgment well. No matter how hard we try, we can't seem to keep up with the many family issues and problems we face. Our frequent lapses challenge our self-esteem and often lead to discouragement.

Despite this inner unrest, my wife usually appears to plow on serenely, so people come up to ask her how she runs such a large family. "How do you manage diapers, play dates, homework, music lessons, college applications, and wedding receptions all at the same time? Doesn't it drive you crazy?"

In response, I've heard her say, "Frankly, it often does." She then goes on to say that she frequently feels tired and frustrated with the young children and that she's never able to arrange as many play dates as she would like. If she's in a really honest mood, she'll even admit that homework sometimes slips through the cracks and we've been known to miss music lessons altogether. To express her frustration, I've even heard her say, "The fact is, I come up short so often that I often feel like Jonah at the bottom of the ocean in the belly of a fish."

Like my wife, we all have moments in which we feel like Jonah. But when we do, it's encouraging to recognize that Jonah didn't perish in that belly. As my wife goes on to point out, Jonah called out to the Lord to save him from his ocean tomb, and when he did, the Lord reached down to pull him out of the deep and bring him safely to shore.

Likewise, each of us can call out to the Lord for help whenever we're discouraged and filled with self doubt. Christ's power to heal is not only deeper than our deepest pain, but it's also greater than our greatest shortcoming. If we have the faith to call out to him, Christ can conquer all our weaknesses. Just as he delivered Jonah from three days of darkness in the belly of a fish, and just as he delivered himself from three days of darkness in the tomb, so Christ can deliver us from our sins, mistakes, and weaknesses.

Hence the commandment to judge not that ye be not judged extends beyond the judgments we may impose on others to the judgments we may impose on ourselves. In fact, even Christ's commandment to be perfect even as our Father in Heaven is perfect isn't a commandment to put our personal sense of worth at stake as we try to become perfect parents, perfect spouses, perfect students, or otherwise perfect people. We can rest assured that as we submit ourselves to Christ, he will gradually build that type of perfection into us, from year to year and on into eternity. Instead, the Lord's commandment to be perfect actually wraps up his discussion on forgiveness, which he delivered during the Sermon on the Mount. Therefore, the commandment to be perfect is to a large degree a commandment to break down our walls of unrighteous judgment and to replace those walls with bridges of forgiveness and love.

Indeed, forgiveness can be viewed as the crowning sacrifice we can place on the altar of God. It complements and completes our submission of all judgment unto him. As we place our valid claims for justice upon his altar, he who was betrayed and scorned himself receives our humble gifts of forgiveness with deep gratitude. As he does, we feel his love and begin to find our esteem in Christ rather than trying to find it in ourselves. That is, we find Christ within us, our truest self, who stands firm against the many attacks upon our sense of worth.

This discovery of the Light of Christ within us is a great adventure. We all can experience it by looking beyond our walls of judgment to the promises he offers unto us. As for me, I feel as if I caught a tangible glimpse of these promises on that day I stood on the Great Wall that wound its way through the rocks and hills of the Middle Kingdom. At first, I peered in toward Beijing, the heart of China. I reflected on the protection the wall had provided, as well as the grim costs of its construction and the isolation it produced, wondering how the country would have been different without it.

I then turned to the north, to the land where the barbarian tribes once lived, and I began to see rich, new horizons. There were fascinating mountains and hills that begged for exploring, stunning blue skies that seemed to stretch on forever, rivers, lakes, and beautiful trees. By looking out beyond that great wall and reaching out to the world beyond, adventure loomed.

Likewise, if we muster the faith to look beyond our own walls of prejudice and unrighteous judgment, crossing bridges to others and to God, adventure looms. Instead of isolation, there will be the joy of companionship—deep, meaningful companionship forged in the bonds of Christ. Instead of loneliness, there will be friendship, not only with others but with God himself. Instead of despair and self-doubt, there will be a profound sense of worth, anchored in the foothold of Christ. Instead of feeling as if we're at the bottom of the sea in the belly of a fish, there will be the overwhelming peace of Christ.

Eventually, the Lord will open new eternal horizons for us to see. There will be fascinating worlds to explore, galaxy upon galaxy. There will be pure rivers of light, trees of everlasting life, and beautiful skies that stretch into infinity. Furthermore, there will be no more walls to separate us from each other in this eternal land of promise; connecting bridges will abound. And among these bridges, our loving Redeemer will stand at the center of this ultimate promised land, filled with joy to see us come home to him.

eight

CAPTAIN OF PEACE

In mid-August, 2005, my wife and I took a short retreat to Camden, Maine. My teaching semester at Tulane University was about to begin, and we wanted to spend some time together before I started the rigorous commute from Connecticut down to Louisiana.

After settling into a bed and breakfast inn, we hiked down to the boardwalk to see the harbor. We found a schooner named *Surprise* and took it for a ride. The crew gave us safety instructions as we taxied out of the harbor and the captain unfurled the sails. We sailed along the shore with ever-increasing speed. In the distance, we could see *Victory Chimes*, one of Maine's most commemorated sailboats. We quickly outpaced her, catching an especially strong wind along the shore.

After a while we gained so much speed that the captain's wife remarked they had never had a run like this before, not in all of their nineteen years of sailing the *Surprise* together. At that point, the boat leaned so far over onto its side that water came pouring onto the deck. I held on to the railing as tightly as I could, trying to stay above the flood.

I became alarmed and wanted to know how the captain was going to right the ship, but when I looked at him he was calm and at ease. Still uneasy myself, I asked him what we should do. He simply answered, "There is no way this wind will knock over the ship—there are fifteen thousand pounds of ballast down at the keel—so you can relax and enjoy the ride." He spoke with confidence, enough confidence that I began to trust in him, even though my senses didn't agree. As I trusted him I felt peace. In the end, we arrived back in the harbor safe and sound.

Since that day, I've reflected back upon this captain and his words many times. Although the winds we faced off the coast of Maine were very strong, the winds we all face in this life sometimes can feel much more powerful and threatening. Temptation, pain, and loss beset us all. When they do, it can be hard to hold on.

At such times there is only one ultimate source of comfort, one foundation for our peace—the comfort and peace of knowing we don't sail alone. We have a captain who has sailed rough waters before, a Prince of Peace who is unruffled by even the most treacherous of storms. He sits at the helm and with absolute confidence promises that he can guide us through the wind and rain.

As I watch the events that are unfolding in the world, it's evident we all will need this strength from our eternal Captain during upcoming years, perhaps like never before. Natural disasters and deadly diseases abound, and Satan is pushing forward a great tide of terror and wickedness upon the entire earth. All of us need an anchor of strength and security, a foundation so strong it will endure through all opposition and grief. We need a foundation forged in eternity—Jesus Christ.

About a week after Kristin and I went to Maine for our retreat, I stood before the new master's of accounting students at

Tulane University. It was Wednesday, August 24, and I spoke at their orientation. There were many more students than there had been the year before, and they were excited to start the school year. I spoke of the effort required to succeed in a graduate program, and I spoke of the integrity required to succeed in the accounting profession.

On Thursday, August 25, I spoke at orientation for the new MBA students. It was a large, diverse class. Just as I was ready to enter the room to speak, I ran into Scott Cowen, the president of the university. He expressed enthusiasm over the entering class and conveyed optimism about the upcoming year.

On Friday, August 26, I left campus for a day to go teach in Tulane's executive MBA program in Houston. I parked my rental car in the lot near the airport in New Orleans and climbed onto a Southwest flight to Houston. Class went well Friday night, but then I began to hear stories about a storm that had entered the gulf, a storm that could make its way to Louisiana. However, I went to bed without too much concern. I still planned to return to New Orleans the next afternoon.

When I went to bed, I couldn't sleep. I began to think more and more about the storm. For three or four hours I did nothing but toss and turn. I couldn't understand why the storm troubled me so much. After all, I had survived the Sylmar earthquake on February 9, 1971, living right next to its epicenter. I had endured the great earthquake of San Francisco on October 17, 1989, a quake that brought down part of the Bay Bridge and postponed the World Series. Still, something about this particular storm seemed especially ominous to me.

Finally, at one o'clock Saturday morning, I couldn't stand the sense of concern any longer, so I left my hotel room and went over to Tulane's Houston facilities. I got online and tried to plan a way to get out of New Orleans once I returned, just in case the storm came through there.

After teaching Saturday morning, I could see even more clearly that New Orleans might be in the path of the storm. I wanted to go back to the city to return my rental car and to gather my belongings, but the sense of dread continued. Finally, this feeling became so strong that I paid several hundred dollars to buy a ticket straight home to Connecticut, yielding up my car and personal belongings to the storm.

On Monday morning, Katrina came ashore, slamming into Louisiana and Mississippi. At first it seemed New Orleans received only a glancing blow. Eventually, however, the levee broke and a flood inundated the city. Like much of the nation, I then watched the events in New Orleans unfold day by day—the abandoned masses at the convention center, the overcrowded Superdome, the looting, the fires, the deaths, and the filthy water. On one newscast I saw a pickup truck largely submerged in the flood waters just around the corner from my apartment.

During the days following Katrina, I went to my knees several times. I was concerned about many colleagues and friends in New Orleans whom I hadn't been able to contact since the storm. With the university that employed me now underwater, I also became concerned about my position at Tulane. Each time I went to my knees, I remained confused; Tulane's future, and my friends' future, remained unclear. Each time I prayed, however, I saw an image in my mind's eye—the image of the captain of the *Surprise.*

No matter how hard the wind blew that day in Maine, he remained calm and at ease. No matter how high the waves rose, he remained confident and sure. With fifteen thousand pounds of ballast at the keel of his ship, he was unruffled by the storm.

As I reflected back on his image, my confidence increased. I still didn't know what I should do, but I did know I wasn't alone. There was a Captain of Peace in my life, a Captain who offers to sit at the helm of each of our lives—Jesus Christ.

Looking back, I find it incredible that Katrina lingered in New Orleans for only a few hours, for her long-term effects were devastating. At Tulane, the damage was so great that we had to cancel the entire fall school semester. Students scattered to a host of other universities, and Tulane fought desperately to survive by keeping as much of the tuition revenue as possible.

Eventually, I learned that some of my colleagues and friends lost everything they owned. Like the students, they scattered to all parts of the country. My second-story apartment stood above the flood, but the wind blew out my air conditioner along with one of the windows, and filthy water flooded the floor below me. It took weeks for anyone to recover my rental car, and even longer for me to get back any of my belongings.

Given this devastation in New Orleans, we had to move the nerve center of the university to Houston, near the Galleria Mall. We set up shop on the sixth and ninth floors of 1700 West Loop South, and as a business school we planned a Saturday full of meetings there. However, those meetings never took place because Rita entered the gulf, yet another powerful storm.

Feeling chased by storm after storm, I couldn't help but think these storms are a prelude to the difficult times that lie ahead, not only for me but for all of us. Therefore, I've given a lot of thought to the measures we might take to prepare for these times.

Temporally, it would be prudent to gather emergency supplies of food and water in our homes, supplies that will sustain us if storms or global disease eventually drive us into our homes for long-term protection. Financially, it would be prudent to build up emergency supplies of cash and assets, supplies that will sustain us through tough times in which the economy may falter.

Most of all, it would be prudent to prepare spiritually, garnering rich supplies of the Light of Christ, the light Christ bestows upon those who turn their lives over to him in faith and obedience, the only light that can shine with courage and hope through the darkest of nights. Like the children of Israel who placed the mark of the lamb's blood upon their doors to protect them from the destroying angel, we need a mark of faith and obedience upon our homes as well.

This mark of faith and obedience is real, and it has power. When the Twin Towers crashed to the ground in New York, I was deeply disturbed. As a professor at Columbia University at the time, I had hundreds of former students working in the area, so I anxiously scoured the lists of the missing. Eventually, I took the subway ride from the Upper West Side of Manhattan, where I worked, down to Ground Zero.

The devastation was tremendous. Not only had the explosions toppled the two great towers, but the falling bricks and debris severely damaged the surrounding buildings, some that were blocks away. Amazingly, however, little St. Paul's chapel remained unscathed. It was just across the street from the Twin Towers, but not even a window was broken. It withstood the attack, standing firm and true.

This was the place where George Washington knelt in prayer just after he was inaugurated as the first president of the United States, a place where thousands have knelt before God over the centuries. It is, I believe, a sacred place, a place with the mark of faith and obedience upon its doors. As I entered this small chapel, I felt reverence and peace: reverence for the protecting care God had bestowed upon this small tabernacle, and peace for the assurance that life extends beyond the veil.

As I circled the halls of the chapel and read the heartfelt memorials to those who passed away, the peace of this assurance of life after death utterly overwhelmed me, erasing all doubt. The Spirit testified that Jesus is the Christ, the literal Son of God, born of the virgin Mary, and the only name under heaven through which we can be saved. It testified that we are eternal beings, beings that emerge from God and eventually return to God, our true home. It testified that there is a tabernacle of peace in our hearts, a place of deep intrinsic worth, founded by Christ himself.

I often find myself thinking of this tabernacle of peace when I sit down to work at the desk in my office at home. There is a large picture of the Savior hanging on the wall in front of me. In this picture, Christ is sitting on a rocky hillside above the city of Jerusalem. It's near sunset, so the shadows are long and the clouds have taken on a golden hue. Christ is alone, looking out over the Kidron Valley toward Jerusalem. The Garden of Gethsemane is just out of my view, but from where the Savior sits he should be able to see it well.

In this picture, Christ is in a reflective mood. I imagine that he is contemplating his love for the city as well as his concern for the destruction he knows awaits it. I also imagine he is contemplating the great sacrifice he is about to make for us. From his vantage point, he can see the spot in Gethsemane where he will soon kneel in blood and tears to take our pain and sins upon him. He can see the court where men will scourge him and place a crown of thorns upon his head. He can see the street where he will soon struggle under the weight of the cross. He may even be able to see Golgotha itself, the place of the skull, the place where he will die for men. Despite this knowledge of his great imminent sacrifice, he is calm and at ease. He seems unruffled by the impending storm.

Continuing to gaze at the picture, I've wondered where he gets such strength to face an infinite sacrifice. To some degree, this strength probably comes from his hillside view of the tomb where he will lay—the tomb from which he knows he will rise on the third day. Seeing through the pain, he perceives the eternal joy of his resurrection beyond it. Mostly, though, this strength I see in him simply comes from within, for his light is the source of power and strength for the entire universe and of peace for all of our trials.

My parents gave this picture to me just after my colleagues voted me out of Columbia University. The inscription at the bottom reads, "Trust in the Lord with all thine heart, and lean not unto thine own understanding, and He shall direct thy paths." I've spent many hours looking at this picture, and many hours thinking about this inscription.

On that cold December night I walked down to the frozen pond behind my home to ask for career guidance after I lost my position at Columbia, I eventually returned to my office, where I sat at my desk and looked up at this image of Christ and read the inscription.

As I read the inscription, it sealed and perfected the experience on the pond for me. While standing on the pond, I had heard the whispers of eternity testify that God is there, he heard my prayer, and he loved me. While sitting at my desk looking at the picture of Christ, I heard the whispers testify that if I would place my trust in the Lord, he would restore my loss a hundred fold and more.

I wish I could say I then trusted in him completely, without an ounce of reservation, but I can't. The pain of rejection was still too fresh, so the best I could do was to trust in part. Yet even trusting in part was enough for him to bestow his peace upon me. With this peace came gratitude, and with the gratitude came a deeper appreciation for the redemption of Christ. In a small way, I think I more fully understood what it means to find our esteem in Christ rather than to find our esteem in the world.

As I write these concluding words, I have this picture of Christ in front of me. It's a beautiful October day in Newtown, Connecticut.

The leaves are beginning to turn gold, red, and orange, and the sky is deep blue. I went jogging earlier this morning and felt the breeze on my face.

The beauty and peace I feel today are so real they're almost tangible. Furthermore, Hurricane Katrina and Hurricane Rita are now behind us, and the city of New Orleans is slowly beginning to come back to life. At Tulane, we are planning to open the university for our students in the spring, and I am scheduled to begin teaching in January.

However, when I check the computer on my desk, I see there's another storm brewing down in the Caribbean. Her name is Wilma, and the National Hurricane Center has just upgraded her from a tropical storm to a hurricane. She will not be the last. As one who has recently returned from New Orleans, I testify that there are many storms on the horizon—storms of wind and rain, storms of tremors and disease, storms of terror, temptation, and sin.

In so testifying, I am not saying anything new. The Lord himself testified of such. I am emphasizing, however, what each of us knows deep down in our hearts—we will all face tough times, and in these times we need the seal and protection of Christ upon us.

With this seal we will not be alone. When waves crash down upon us, waves so strong that it will be hard to hold on, Christ will be standing there next to us in the surf. He will be ready to reach into the waves to pull us out. No matter how deep our pain, he will be there to find us in the surf and to command the waves to be at peace and to be still.

When he does, he will pull us up into his arms, where his power to heal is deeper than our deepest pain. In these arms, it will not matter how hard the wind may blow during upcoming years, for ever before us we will have the image of our eternal Captain of Peace—Jesus Christ. We will feel his love and know his strength, and he will bring us back to the harbor safe and sound, back to our eternal home.

God is there, he hears your prayers, and he loves you.

About the Author

Deen Kemsley is the Exxon Professor of Accounting at Tulane University. He also conducts training programs for stock and bond analysts on Wall Street. He has published extensively in premier business journals, and his research has played an important role in national debates on taxes, dividends, and debt. In addition, he has earned top teaching awards at Columbia and Tulane, and his students at Yale have honored him for his superb lectures. Most of all, however, he loves the Lord, so for many years he has looked forward to applying his teaching talents to the witness of Jesus Christ.

Deen and his wife, Kristin, are the parents of nine children. They live in rural Newtown, Connecticut, and Deen often speaks of Christ to congregations throughout parts of Connecticut and New York.